MERMAIDS, SIRENS AND SELKIES

Myths and Legends

More classic literature available from
Macmillan Collector's Library

Fairies, Elves and Sprites

Witches, Wizards and Sorcerers

Dragons, Wyverns and Serpents

Greek Myths: Gods and Goddesses

Greek Myths: Heroes and Heroines

The Odyssey by Homer

The Iliad by Homer

The Aeneid by Virgil

MERMAIDS, SIRENS AND SELKIES

Myths and Legends

Edited and introduced by
JEAN MENZIES

MACMILLAN COLLECTOR'S LIBRARY

This collection first published 2025 by Macmillan Collector's Library
an imprint of Pan Macmillan
The Smithson, 6 Briset Street, London EC1M 5NR
EU representative: Macmillan Publishers Ireland Ltd,
1st Floor, The Liffey Trust Centre, 117-126 Sheriff Street Upper,
Dublin 1, DO1 YC43
Associated companies throughout the world
www.panmacmillan.com

ISBN 978-1-0350-3161-0

Introductions copyright © Jean Menzies 2025
Selection and arrangement copyright © Macmillan Publishers
International Ltd. 2025

'Pania of The Reef' by Tuiri Tareha, first published in *Te Ao Hou*, 1955.

All rights reserved. No part of this publication may be reproduced,
stored in a retrieval system, or transmitted, in any form, or by any means
(electronic, mechanical, photocopying, recording or otherwise)
without the prior written permission of the publisher.

3 5 7 9 8 6 4 2

A CIP catalogue record for this book is available from the British Library.

Endpaper pattern by Andrew Davidson
Typeset in Plantin by Jouve (UK), Milton Keynes
Printed and bound in China by Imago

This book is sold subject to the condition that it shall not, by way of
trade or otherwise, be lent, hired out, or otherwise circulated without
the publisher's prior consent in any form of binding or cover other than
that in which it is published and without a similar condition including
this condition being imposed on the subsequent purchaser.

Visit **www.panmacmillan.com** to read more
about all our books and to buy them.

Contents

Introduction vii

THE MERMAN 1
Jón Árnason

THE HORNED SERPENT 6
Arthur Caswell Parker

LEGEND OF MELUSINA 14
Thomas Keightley

THE MERMAID WIFE 20
Thomas Keightley

THE NIX IN THE POND 25
Brothers Grimm tr. Charles Folkard

THE SEA-MAIDEN 35
Stephen Jones and B. L. K. Henderson

THE MERMAID AND THE BOY 50
Andrew Lang

THE SHARK MAN 69
Thomas G. Thrum

FLORY CANTILLON'S FUNERAL 86
Thomas Crofton Croker

THE MERMAID 94
Hanashika

THE SEAL CATCHER AND THE
MERMAN 101
Elizabeth Grierson

THE WANDERING OF ODYSSEUS 112
Josephine Preston Peabody

PANIA OF THE REEF 122
Tuiri Tareha

THE ENCHANTED FISH 125
Andrew Lang

THE TUNA (EEL) OF LAKE VAIHIRIA 142
Teuria Henry

GLAUCUS AND SCYLLA 151
Emily Kip Baker

THE LITTLE MERMAID 156
Hans Christian Andersen

Introduction
JEAN MENZIES

With 71 per cent of the earth's surface made up of oceans – oceans that measure more than 10,000 metres at their deepest point, but which we have only explored a mere 5 per cent of thus far – is it any wonder that we are fascinated by the sea, and what might be out there?* For millennia, cultures around the world have speculated as to what mysterious creatures might live beneath the waves, in caverns, along coasts, and even in their local loch (cough, Nessie, cough).

Babylonian mythology featured wise fish-men called Uanna, who simultaneously possessed the tail of a fish and human feet so they could wander around on land before going for a swim. The Assyrians, according to Diodorus Siculus, worshiped Atargatis, a goddess whose body was partly transformed into a fish when, out of shame and grief for killing her lover and child, she threw herself into a lake. Meanwhile, the Ancient Greeks celebrated Triton, son of the god Poseidon, whose

* https://oceanexplorer.noaa.gov/facts/explored.html (accessed June 2024)

lower body was variously depicted as one fish tail, two fish tails, and even a lobster.

But of course, the sea, with its dangerous depths, wicked waves and treacherous temperatures, must be home to more than just deities and wisemen. While many modern mermaids might be friendly and kind, even desperate to be 'a part of our world', the mermaids of lore are often reflections of humanity's own rather difficult relationship with the sea, luring sailors and fishermen to their deaths either on the rocks by the shore or beneath the water itself.

But what exactly is a mermaid? Or merperson should I say. The word 'mere' comes from the Old English and can refer to various bodies of water including seas, lakes, pools, and ponds – inside all of which you might find creatures akin to merfolk. So, essentially, a person of the water. In reality, the term itself says nothing in particular about how said merfolk look, and yet there is no denying that the popular image of a merperson is a creature with the tail of a fish and body of a human – whether it be man or woman.

From the ancient walls of Pompeii to the pages of eleventh-century Japanese newspapers, from the margins of medieval English bestiaries to the dioramas of twenty-first-century theme parks,

mermaids are, and seemingly always have been, all around us. So much so that they have frequently broken free of their mythological confines and made their way into our everyday lives.

For example, you might have heard of the 'Fiji Mermaid': the mummified creature of disputed origin, half monkey, half fish, sewn together and displayed to the public as part of P. T. Barnum's infamous 'Museum'. But did you know that the Roman naturalist Pliny wrote of scale-covered nereids and tritons (not the god, it seems) washing up on the shores of Spain and Portugal? Or that a mummified 'mermaid' held by a temple in the Okayama Prefecture of Japan was only recently shown to be made up of various materials including a pufferfish skin?

While these modern mermaids have since been outed as hoaxes, it is clear that as humans we remain constantly on alert for any sign of these magical creatures. So much so that organizations such as NOAA (the National Oceanic and Atmospheric Administration, in the US) have had to publish disclaimers on their website that no evidence of mermaids exists.* To put it simply: we are enamoured.

---

* https://oceanservice.noaa.gov/facts/mermaids.html (accessed June 2024)

Regardless of what you choose to believe, however, there is no denying mermaids (and their kin) their cultural and historical significance. Early modern maps are littered with illustrations of these fishy women alongside various monsters of the deep, serving to demarcate mysterious lands and uncharted waters. Distinctly tempting despite the danger they pose, the mermaid has acted as a visual and oral representation of the myriad dangers faced by humans at sea – whether it be the lure of the sirens' call or simply the unforgiving nature of the currents.

Mermaids are as much a mystery as the 95 per cent of the oceans we have yet to explore, a reflection of our tumultuous relationship with the world's watery depths throughout history, a relationship that never fails to pull us back. To imagine that all legendary creatures of the water must appear the same, therefore, is to truly limit the possibilities of such a vast and murky world. So, don't be surprised if in these stories of 'merfolk' from around the world you meet those with serpentine and avian lower halves; those who don seal skins before they dive beneath the waves; those with the capacity to transform into sharks and eels; those who look deceptively human in their entirety; and just some good old-fashioned talking fish.

MERMAIDS, SIRENS AND SELKIES

Myths and Legends

THE MERMAN

Why not counter your expectations by opening a volume entitled *Mermaids, Sirens and Selkies* with a story of, instead, a merman? The following tale of 'The Merman' comes from *Icelandic Legends*, a collection of folk-tales compiled by nineteenth-century folklorist Jón Árnason, who is often credited with publishing the first ever collection of Icelandic folk-tales – a contribution this volume must surely be grateful for. Translated here by George E. J. Powell and Eiríkur Magnússon, this story of the merman is one that reminds us to be kind to the sea and the creatures within it. This at least is the lesson the fisherman at the centre of the story must learn, and is it not therefore an excellent lesson with which to begin this collection? It is also one which, I hope, stands regardless of whether or not said magical creature can offer you gifts of gold or cattle.

Long ago a farmer lived at Vogar, who was a mighty fisherman, and, of all the farms round about, not one was so well situated with regard to the fisheries as his.

One day, according to custom, he had gone out fishing, and having cast down his line from the boat, and waited awhile, found it very hard to pull up again, as if there were something very heavy at the end of it. Imagine his astonishment when he found that what he had caught was a great fish, with a man's head and body! When he saw that this creature was alive, he addressed it and said, "Who and whence are you?"

"A merman from the bottom of the sea," was the reply.

The farmer then asked him what he had been doing when the hook caught his flesh.

The other replied, "I was turning the cowl of my mother's chimney-pot, to suit it to the wind. So let me go again, will you?"

"Not for the present," said the fisherman. "You shall serve me awhile first."

So without more words he dragged him into the boat and rowed to shore with him.

When they got to the boat-house, the fisherman's dog came to him and greeted him joyfully, barking and fawning on him, and wagging his tail. But his master's temper being none of the best, he struck the poor animal; whereupon the merman laughed for the first time.

Having fastened the boat, he went towards his house, dragging his prize with him, over the fields, and stumbling over a hillock, which lay in his way, cursed it heartily; whereupon the merman laughed for the second time.

When the fisherman arrived at the farm, his wife came out to receive him, and embraced him affectionately, and he received her salutations with pleasure; whereupon the merman laughed for the third time.

Then said the farmer to the merman, "You have laughed three times, and I am curious to know *why* you have laughed. Tell me, therefore."

"Never will I tell you," replied the merman, "unless you promise to take me to the same place in the sea wherefrom you caught me, and there to

let me go free again." So the farmer made him the promise.

"Well," said the merman, "I laughed the first time because you struck your dog, whose joy at meeting you was real and sincere. The second time, because you cursed the mound over which you stumbled, which is full of golden ducats. And the third time, because you received with pleasure your wife's empty and flattering embrace, who is faithless to you, and a hypocrite. And now be an honest man and take me out to the sea whence you have brought me."

The farmer replied: "Two things that you have told me I have no means of proving, namely, the faithfulness of my dog and the faithlessness of my wife. But the third I will try the truth of, and if the hillock contain gold, then I will believe the rest."

Accordingly he went to the hillock, and having dug it up, found therein a great treasure of golden ducats, as the merman had told him. After this the farmer took the merman down to the boat, and to that place in the sea whence he had caught him. Before he put him in, the latter said to him:

"Farmer, you have been an honest man, and I will reward you for restoring me to my mother, if only you have skill enough to take possession of

property that I shall throw in your way. Be happy and prosper."

Then the farmer put the merman into the sea, and he sank out of sight.

It happened that not long after, seven sea-grey cows were seen on the beach, close to the farmer's land. These cows appeared to be very unruly, and ran away directly the farmer approached them. So he took a stick and ran after them, possessed with the fancy that if he could burst the bladder which he saw on the nose of each of them, they would belong to him. He contrived to hit out the bladder on the nose of one cow, which then became so tame that he could easily catch it, while the others leaped into the sea and disappeared. The farmer was convinced that this was the gift of the merman. And a very useful gift it was, for better cow was never seen nor milked in all the land, and she was the mother of the race of grey cows so much esteemed now.

And the farmer prospered exceedingly, but never caught any more mermen. As for his wife, nothing further is told about her, so we can repeat nothing.

THE HORNED SERPENT

While you will find that many of the tales in this collection feature women of the sea, who either lure sailors to their sides or else are whisked away as their brides, both willingly and unwillingly, this next story is one in which the human tempted by a mysterious creature of the water is instead a woman who is ignorant of her mysterious husband's true identity. The tale of 'The Horned Serpent' (or 'The Horned Serpent Runs Away with the Girl Who is Rescued by the Thunderer') belongs to the indigenous American people of the Seneca Nation, one of the six Iroquois nations. The story as it is told here was preserved by the twentieth-century historian and folklorist Arthur Caswell Parker – who himself was a member of the Seneca nation – in his collection *Seneca Myths and Folk Tales*. It also features Hé-no, an Iroquois thunder spirit.

There was a Thunderer named Hi"no" who often hovered about a village where he sought to attract the attention of a certain young woman. He was a very friendly man and would have nothing to do with witches. He hated all kinds of sorcery and his great chief up in the sky whom we call Grandfather Thunder hated all wizardry and sorcery too. All the Thunderers killed witches when they could find them at their evil work.

Now, this Hi"no" was very sure that he would win the girl he wanted and he visited her lodge at night and took a fire brand from the fire and sat down and talked with her, but she kept saying, "Not yet, perhaps by and by."

Hi"no" was puzzled and resolved to watch for the coming of a rival. He told the girl's father that he suspected some witch had cast a spell on her or that some wizard was secretly visiting her. So they both watched.

That same night a strange man came. He had a very fine suit of clothing, and the skin had a

peculiar tan. It was very clean, as if washed so that it shone with a glitter. Over his back and down the center there was a broad stripe of black porcupine quills with a small diamond-shaped pattern. He had a long neck and small beady eyes, but he was graceful and moved without noise. He went directly to the lodge and taking a light sat at the girl's bedside.

"Are you willing?" he asked her. "Come now, let us depart. I want you for my wife. I will take you to my house."

The girl replied, "Not yet, I think someone is watching, but in three days I will be ready."

The next day the girl worked very hard making a new dress and spent much time putting black porcupine quills upon it as an ornamentation. It was her plan to have a dress that would match her lover's suit. Upon the third day she finished her work and went to bed early. Her apartment was at the right side of the door and it was covered by a curtain of buffalo skin that hung all the way down.

Hi″ no″ again called upon her, taking a light and seating himself back of the curtain. "I am willing to marry you," he said. "When will you become my wife?"

"Not yet," she replied. "I am not ready now to marry."

"I think you are deceiving me," answered Hi"no", "for you have on your new dress and have not removed your moccasins."

"You may go," the girl told him, and he went away.

Soon there came the stranger and he too took a little torch and went behind the curtain. Soon the two came out together and ran down the path to the river.

"I shall take you now to my own tribe," said the lover. "We live only a short way from here. We must go over the hill."

So onward they went to their home, at length arriving at the high rocky shores of a lake. They stood on the edge of the cliff and looked down at the water.

"I see no village and no house," complained the girl. "Where shall we go now? I am sure that we are pursued by the Thunderer."

As she said this the Thunderer and the girl's father appeared running toward them.

"It is dark down there," said the lover. "We will now descend and find our house."

So saying he took the girl by the waist and crawled down the cliff, suddenly diving with a splash into the lake. Down they went until they reached the foot of the cliff, when an opening

appeared into which he swam with her. Quickly he swam upward and soon they were in a dimly lighted lodge. It was a strange place and filled with numerous fine things. All along the wall there were different suits of clothing.

"Look at all the suits," said the lover, "when you have found one put it on."

That night the couple were married and the next day the husband went away. "I shall return in three days," he announced. "Examine the fine things here, and when you find a dress that you like put it on."

For a long time the girl looked at the things in the lodge, but she was afraid to put on anything for everything had such a fishy smell. There was one dress, however, that attracted the girl and she was tempted to put it on. It was very long and had a train. It was covered all over with decorations that looked like small porcupine quills flattened out. There was a hood fastened to it and to the hood was fastened long branching antlers. She looked at this dress longingly but hung it up again with a sigh, for it smelled like fish and she was afraid.

In due time her husband returned and asked her if she had selected a suit. "I have found one that I admire greatly," said she. "But I am afraid

that I will not like it after I put it on. It has a peculiar fishy smell and I am afraid that it may bring evil upon me if I wear it."

"Oh no!" exclaimed her husband, "If you wear that suit I will be greatly pleased. It is the very suit that I hoped you would select. Put it on, my wife, put it on, for then I shall be greatly pleased. When I return from my next trip I hope you will wear it for me."

The next day the husband went away, again promising soon to return. Again the girl busied herself with looking at the trophies hanging in the lodge. She noticed that there were many suits like the one she had admired. Carefully she examined each and then it dawned upon her that these garments were the clothing of great serpents. She was horrified at the discovery and resolved to escape. As she went to the door she was swept back by a wave. She tried the back door but was forced into the lodge again by the water. Finally mustering all her courage she ran out of the door and jumped upward. She knew that she had been in a house under water. Soon she came to the surface but it was dark and there were thunder clouds in the sky. A great storm was coming up. Then she heard a great splashing and through the water she saw a monster serpent plowing his way toward her. Its

eyes were fiercely blazing and there were horns upon its head. As it came toward her she scrambled in dismay up the dark slippery rocks to escape it. As the lightning flashed she looked sharply at the creature and saw that its eyes were those of her husband. She noticed in particular a certain mark on his eyes that had before strangely fascinated her. Then she realized that this was her husband and that he was a great horned serpent.

She screamed and sought to scale the cliff with redoubled vigor, but the monster was upon her with a great hiss. His huge bulk coiled to embrace her, when there was a terrific peal of thunder, a blinding flash, and the serpent fell dead, stricken by one of Hi"˝no"˝'s arrows.

The girl was about to fall when a strong arm grasped her and bore her away in the darkness, Soon she was back at her father's lodge. The Thunderer had rescued her.

"I wanted to save you," he said, "but the great horned serpent kept me away by his magic. He stole you and took you to his home. It is important that you answer me one question: did you ever put on any dress that he gave you? If you did you are no longer a woman but a serpent."

"I resisted the desire to put on the garment," she told him.

"Then," said he, "you must go to a sweat lodge and be purified."

The girl went to the women's sweat lodge and they prepared her for the purification. When she had sweat and been purged with herbs, she gave a scream and all the women screamed for she had expelled two young serpents, and they ran down and slipped off her feet. The Thunderer outside killed them with a loud noise.

After a while the young woman recovered and told all about her adventure, and after a time the Thunderer came to her lodge and said, "I would like to take you now."

"I will give you some bread," she answered, meaning that she wished to marry him. So she gave him some bread which he ate and then they were married.

The people of the village were now all afraid that the lake would be visited by horned serpents seeking revenge but the Thunderer showed them a medicine bag filled with black scales, and he gave every warrior who would learn his song one scale, and it was a scale from the back of the horned serpent. He told them that if they wore this scale, the serpent could not harm them. So, there are those scales in medicine bundles to this day.

LEGEND OF MELUSINA

Meet Melusina, also known as Melusine. Melusina is a figure who appears across various European mythological traditions, including in France, Luxembourg (where you'll find her statue along the edge of the river Alzette), and Germany; she is also the perfect example of how it is often difficult to distinguish mermaids and the like from fairies more generally (you can check out the fairy volume in this series for more fairies). It is perhaps no surprise therefore that she proved a subject of interest to Thomas Keightley, who included the following rendition of her tale in his nineteenth-century collection *The Fairy Mythology*. Keightley for his part was particularly interested in the comparative study of folklore – drawing parallels between similar tales from around the world. So, while this is a great place to start, why not read another version of Melusina's tale once you're done?

Elinas, king of Albania, to divert his grief for the death of his wife, amused himself with hunting. One day, at the chase, he went to a fountain to quench his thirst: as he approached it he heard the voice of a woman singing, and on coming to it he found there the beautiful Fay Pressina.

After some time the Fay bestowed her hand upon him, on the condition that he should never visit her at the time of her lying-in. She had three daughters at a birth: Melusina, Melior, and Palatina. Nathas, the king's son by a former wife, hastened to convey the joyful tidings to his father, who, without reflection, flew to the chamber of the queen, and entered as she was bathing her daughters. Pressina, on seeing him, cried out that he had broken his word, and she must depart; and taking up her three daughters, she disappeared.

She retired to the Lost Island; so called because it was only by chance any, even those who had repeatedly visited it, could find it. Here she reared her children, taking them every morning to a high

mountain, whence Albania might be seen, and telling them that but for their father's breach of promise they might have lived happily in the distant land which they beheld. When they were fifteen years of age, Melusina asked her mother particularly of what their father had been guilty. On being informed of it, she conceived the design of being revenged on him. Engaging her sisters to join in her plans, they set out for Albania: arrived there, they took the king and all his wealth, and, by a charm, inclosed him in a high mountain, called Brandelois. On telling their mother what they had done, she, to punish them for the unnatural action, condemned Melusina to become every Saturday a serpent, from the waist downwards, till she should meet a man who would marry her under the condition of never seeing her on a Saturday, and should keep his promise. She inflicted other judgements on her two sisters, less severe in proportion to their guilt. Melusina now went roaming through the world in search of the man who was to deliver her. She passed through the Black Forest, and that of Ardennes, and at last she arrived in the forest of Colombiers, in Poitou, where all the Fays of the neighbourhood came before her, telling her they had been waiting for her to reign in that place.

Raymond having accidentally killed the count,

his uncle, by the glancing aside of his boar-spear, was wandering by night in the forest of Colombiers. He arrived at a fountain that rose at the foot of a high rock. This fountain was called by the people the Fountain of Thirst, or the Fountain of the Fays, on account of the many marvellous things which had happened at it. At the time, when Raymond arrived at the fountain, three ladies were diverting themselves there by the light of the moon, the principal of whom was Melusina. Her beauty and her amiable manners quickly won his love: she soothed him, concealed the deed he had done, and married him, he promising on his oath never to desire to see her on a Saturday. She assured him that a breach of his oath would for ever deprive him of her whom he so much loved, and be followed by the unhappiness of both for life. Out of her great wealth, she built for him, in the neighbourhood of the Fountain of Thirst, where he first saw her, the castle of Lusignan. She also built La Rochelle, Cloitre Malliers, Mersent, and other places.

But destiny, that would have Melusina single, was incensed against her. The marriage was made unhappy by the deformity of the children born of one that was enchanted; but still Raymond's love for the beauty that ravished both heart and eyes

remained unshaken. Destiny now renewed her attacks. Raymond's cousin had excited him to jealousy and to secret concealment, by malicious suggestions of the purport of the Saturday retirement of the countess. He hid himself; and then saw how the lovely form of Melusina ended below in a snake, gray and sky-blue, mixed with white. But it was not horror that seized him at the sight, it was infinite anguish at the reflection that through his breach of faith he might lose his lovely wife for ever. Yet this misfortune had not speedily come on him, were it not that his son, Geoffroi with the tooth, had burned his brother Freimund, who would stay in the abbey of Malliers, with the abbot and a hundred monks. At which the afflicted father, count Raymond, when his wife Melusina was entering his closet to comfort him, broke out into these words against her, before all the courtiers who attended her:—"Out of my sight, thou pernicious snake and odious serpent! thou contaminator of my race!"

Melusina's former anxiety was now verified, and the evil that had lain so long in ambush had now fearfully sprung on him and her. At these reproaches she fainted away; and when at length she revived, full of the profoundest grief, she declared to him that she must now depart from

him, and, in obedience to a decree of destiny, fleet about the earth in pain and suffering, as a spectre, until the day of doom; and that only when one of her race was to die at Lusignan would she become visible.

Her words at parting were these:

"But one thing will I say unto thee before I part, that thou, and those who for more than a hundred years shall succeed thee, shall know that whenever I am seen to hover over the fair castle of Lusignan, then will it be certain that in that very year the castle will get a new lord; and though people may not perceive me in the air, yet they will see me by the Fountain of Thirst; and thus shall it be so long as the castle stands in honour and flourishing—especially on the Friday before the lord of the castle shall die." Immediately, with wailing and loud lamentation, she left the castle of Lusignan, and has ever since existed as a spectre of the night. Raymond died as a hermit on Monserrat.

THE MERMAID WIFE

The next story tells the tale of the selkie. Variously referred to here as a sea maiden or mermaid, the selkie is a little different from the image of a 'mermaid' you might be most familiar with; for rather than the torso of a woman and the tail of a fish, the selkie is a seal person who can shed their skin to reveal a human form beneath. A popular figure of Scottish folklore, and one of the stories I remember most vividly from my own childhood, the following version of the selkie's tale comes from Thomas Keightley's nineteenth-century collection *The Fairy Mythology*. The author in turn identifies his variation as originating in the Shetland islands, although, as mentioned, various tales of seal folk, both male and female, can be found across Scotland. Another famous selkie, for example, features in the Orkney ballad 'The Silkie of Sule Skerry'.

On a fine summer's evening, an inhabitant of Unst happened to be walking along the sandy margin of a voe. The moon was risen, and by her light he discerned at some distance before him a number of the sea-people, who were dancing with great vigour on the smooth sand. Near them he saw lying on the ground several seal-skins.

As the man approached the dancers, all gave over their merriment, and flew like lightning to secure their garments; then clothing themselves, plunged in the form of seals into the sea. But the Shetlander, on coming up to the spot where they had been, and casting his eyes down on the ground, saw that they had left one skin behind them, which was lying just at his feet. He snatched it up, carried it swiftly away, and placed it in security.

On returning to the shore, he met the fairest maiden that eye ever gazed upon: she was walking backwards and forwards, lamenting in most piteous tones the loss of her seal-skin robe, without which she never could hope to rejoin her family

and friends below the waters, but must remain an unwilling inhabitant of the region enlightened by the sun.

The man approached and endeavoured to console her, but she would not be comforted. She implored him in the most moving accents to restore her dress; but the view of her lovely face, more beautiful in tears, had steeled his heart. He represented to her the impossibility of her return, and that her friends would soon give her up; and finally, made an offer to her of his heart, hand, and fortune.

The sea-maiden, finding she had no alternative, at length consented to become his wife. They were married, and lived together for many years, during which time they had several children, who retained no vestiges of their marine origin, saving a thin web between their fingers, and a bend of their hands, resembling that of the fore paws of a seal; distinctions which characterise the descendants of the family to the present day.

The Shetlander's love for his beautiful wife was unbounded, but she made but a cold return to his affection. Often would she steal out alone and hasten down to the lonely strand, and there at a given signal, a seal of large size would make his appearance, and they would converse for hours

together in an unknown language; and she would return home from this meeting pensive and melancholy.

Thus glided away years, and her hopes of leaving the upper world had nearly vanished, when it chanced one day, that one of the children, playing behind a stack of corn, found a seal-skin. Delighted with his prize, he ran with breathless eagerness to display it before his mother. Her eyes glistened with delight at the view of it; for in it she saw her own dress, the loss of which had cost her so many tears. She now regarded herself as completely emancipated from thraldom; and in idea she was already with her friends beneath the waves. One thing alone was a drawback on her raptures. She loved her children, and she was now about to leave them for ever. Yet they weighed not against the pleasures she had in prospect: so after kissing and embracing them several times, she took up the skin, went out, and proceeded down to the beach.

In a few minutes after the husband came in, and the children told him what had occurred. The truth instantly flashed across his mind, and he hurried down to the shore with all the speed that love and anxiety could give. But he only arrived in time to see his wife take the form of a seal, and from the ledge of a rock plunge into the sea.

The large seal, with whom she used to hold her conversations, immediately joined her, and congratulated her on her escape, and they quitted the shore together. But ere she went she turned round to her husband, who stood in mute despair on the rock, and whose misery excited feelings of compassion in her breast. "Farewell," said she to him, "and may all good fortune attend you. I loved you well while I was with you, but I always loved my first husband better."

The water-spirit is in Shetland called Shoopiltee; he appears in the form of a pretty little horse, and endeavours to entice persons to ride on him, and then gallops with them into the sea.

THE NIX IN THE POND

The nineteenth-century German brothers Jacob and Wilhelm Grimm are two of the most well-known European folklorists today; even if you don't realize it, you're probably familiar with at least one of the stories collected in their fairy tales in some form or another. While you might recognize the figures of Snow White or Hansel and Gretel, I'd wager fewer of you will know the story of 'The Nix in the Pond' – not least because it hasn't yet been adapted into a multitude of films, ballets, and more. This fairy tale tells the story of a man abducted by a nix: a Germanic water spirit popular in European folklore. The nix, or nixie, is also a shapeshifter, sometimes appearing as a horse like the Scottish kelpie, and rising up to drag passers-by into the water. The nix in this tale, however, takes the form of a beautiful woman.

There was once upon a time a Miller who lived very happily with his Wife, for they were very well off, and their prosperity increased year by year. But misfortune comes by night. As their riches had grown, so they disappeared; and thus they melted away yearly till at last the Miller had only his mill, and that he could scarcely call his own property. He became very full of trouble over his losses; and when he lay down after his day's work he could get no rest, but tossed about in his bed, thinking and thinking. One morning he arose before day-break, and went out into the open air, to consider some way of lightening his heart; and as he passed by the mill-dam the first ray of the sun shone forth, and he heard a rippling in the pond. He turned round and perceived a beautiful Maiden, raising herself slowly out of the water. Her long hair, which she had gathered behind her shoulders with her long fingers, fell down on both sides of her face, and covered her white bosom. The Miller saw at once that it was the Nix of the mill-pond, and he knew

not from fear whether to stop or go away. The Nix solved nis doubts by calling him by name in a gentle voice, and asking him why he was so sad. At first the Miller was dumb; but as she spoke so kindly to him, he took courage, and told her that he had once lived in riches and prosperity, but he was now so poor he knew not what to do.

"Rest quietly," said the Nix; "I will make you richer and happier than you were before; only you must promise me that you will give me what has just now been born in your house." "That can be nothing else than a puppy or a kitten," thought the Miller, and so promised the Nix what she desired. Thereupon she dived again under water, and the Miller hastened home to his mill in good spirits. He had almost reached it, when the Maid coming from it met him and told him to rejoice, for his Wife has just borne him a little boy. The Miller started back, as if struck by lightning, for he at once perceived that the crafty Nix was aware of the fact, and had deceived him. He went into his Wife's room drooping his head; and when she inquired why he did not congratulate her on her happiness, he told her what had happened, and the promise which he had given to the Nix. "Of what use are wealth and good luck to me," he continued, "if I lose my child? but what can I do?" And none of the

friends who came to congratulate him on the birth of a son and heir could give any advice.

Meanwhile the luck of the mill returned. What its Master undertook prospered; and it seemed as if chests and coffers filled themselves, for the money in the cupboard increased every night, till before many months had passed away, the Miller was much richer than before. He could not, however, feel any pleasure in the prospect, for his promise to the Nix weighed on his mind; and as often as he passed the pond, he feared lest she should rise and claim her debt. The Boy himself he would never allow to go near the water; but told him continually to beware of doing so, for if he should fall in, a hand would rise and draw him under. Still, as year after year passed away, and the Nix made no second appearance, the Miller began to lose his suspicions.

The Boy grew up a fine youth and was bound to a Huntsman to learn his art, which when he had thoroughly studied, the Lord of the village took him into his service. Now in this village there dwelt a beautiful and good Maiden, who took the fancy of the young Hunter, and when his Master perceived it, he presented him with a small cottage; and thereupon the two married, and lived happily and lovingly together.

One day the Hunter pursued a stag, and when the animal escaped from the forest into the open fields, he followed it, and at last struck it down with a shot from his gun. But he did not observe that he had come to the brink of the dangerous pond, and so when he had flayed his booty, he went to it to wash his hands free from the blood stains. Scarcely had he touched it when the Nix arose, and smilingly embracing him with her naked arms, drew him so quickly below the surface that the water rippled on without a bubble.

By-and-by, when evening came, and the Hunter did not return home, his wife felt very anxious. She went out to seek him; and as he had often told her that he had to take care of the appearance of the Nix, and not venture too near the mill-pond, she suspected already what had happened. She hastened to the water; and as soon as she saw his gun lying on the bank, she could no longer doubt the misfortune which had befallen her. Wringing her hands with grief and terror, she called her beloved by name, but in vain; she hurried from one side of the pond to the other; she alternately entreated and scolded the Nix; but no answer followed—the surface of the water remained as smooth as a mirror, and only the half-crescent of the moon looked up at her fixedly.

The poor Wife could not leave the water. With quick and hasty steps, she walked round and round the pond without cessation, now silent, and now uttering a fearful shriek, and anon a smothered lament. At length her strength forsook her; and sinking to the earth she fell into a deep sleep, and soon a dream passed over her mind.

She thought she was sorrowfully climbing up between great blocks of stone; thorns and nettles pierced her feet, the rain beat in her face, and the wind disordered her long hair. But when she reached the top of the height, quite another aspect appeared. The sky was blue, the air balmy, the ground softy declined; and upon a green meadow, spangled with flowers, stood an elegant cottage. She thought she went up to it and opened the door, and saw an Old Woman with white hair sitting within, who beckoned to her kindly; and at that moment she awoke. The day was already dawning, and the poor Wife determined to follow out her dream. There was a hill close by her, and up this she ascended, and found the road as she had seen in her dream. On the other side stood the cottage, and in it an Old Woman, who kindly received her, and showed her a chair to sit down upon. "You must have suffered some misfortune to induce you to seek my solitary hut," said the Old

Woman. The Wife related to her with tears what had happened; and the Old Woman replied, "Be comforted, I will help you. Here you have a golden comb; wait now till the rising of the full moon; and then go to the pond, and sit down on the bank, and comb your long black hair with it. When you have done, lie down on the bank, and you will see what happens."

The Wife returned, but the time passed very wearisomely till the rise of the moon. At length the shining orb appeared in the sky, and she went down to the pond, and, sitting on its bank, combed her long black hair with the golden comb, and then lay down on the shore to wait the issue. In a short time the waters began to bubble, and a wave rolling on to the bank, carried away with it the comb as it receded. In as much time as was necessary for the sinking of the comb to the bottom, the waters parted, and the head of the Huntsman appeared. He did not speak, but looked at his Wife sorrowfully; and the same moment another wave rolled on and covered his head. All then disappeared, the water became as placid as before, and nothing was to be seen in it but the face of the moon.

The Wife turned back uncomforted, and her dreams again showed the Old Woman's hut. So a second time she travelled up the hill, and laid her

complaint before the Old Woman, who this time gave her a golden flute, with directions to wait till the next full moon, and then to play a sweet tune upon the shore of the pond, and that finished, to lie down and wait the result as before.

The Wife did exactly as the Old Woman told her, and as soon as she laid the flute down, a bubbling took place in the water, and a rising wave carried away the flute. Then appeared not only the head but half of the body of the Man, and stretched out his arms towards his Wife; but at the same instant a wave came, and covering his head, drew him down again.

"Alas! how am I helped," cried the unhappy Wife, "if I see my Husband only to lose him." Grief again overcame her; but in her dreams she visited again the Old Woman's hut. Accordingly she set out on the journey a third time, and received a spinning-wheel of gold from the Old Woman, who comforted her, and told her, "All is not yet complete; wait till the next full moon, and then sit down as before on the shore of the pond and spin your reel full, which done, lay it down near the water and await the result,"

The Wife did everything exactly. As soon as the full moon came she carried her wheel to the shore and spun the reel full; but she had scarcely set it

down against the water than the bubbles began to rise quicker than ever, and a huge wave dashing up carried away with it the spinning-wheel. Immediately afterwards the head and whole body of the Man arose, and he, springing quickly to the shore, caught his Wife by the hand and fled away with her. But they had gone but a little distance, when with a terrible rushing noise the whole pond overflowed its banks, and streamed away into the fields with overwhelming force. The fugitives perceived at once death before their eyes, and in her terror the poor Wife called upon the Old Woman for help, and in a moment they were changed, the one into a Frog and the other into a Toad. The flood which then reached them could not kill them, but it tore them asunder and carried them far away.

When the water subsided again, and the Toad and Frog touched dry ground their human forms returned, but neither knew where the other was, and both were among strange people who knew nothing of their country. High hills and deep valleys lay between them, and in order to earn a livelihood each had to tend sheep; and through many long years they fed their flocks in field and forest, grieving and longing for each other.

When once again spring had covered the earth with its first-fruits, it chanced that both drove their

flocks out the same day, and towards the same point. The former Huntsman perceived on a distant peak of a hill a flock, and drove his sheep to the same place. Thus the two came together in a valley; but, without recognising each other, they were glad that they would have no longer to wander in solitude. From that day they drove their flocks together, and without speaking much, they felt a certain comfort steal over them. One evening when the full moon appeared in the heavens, and the flocks were resting, the Shepherd taking a flute from his pocket, played a soft and mournful air. As he finished he saw that the Shepherdess was weeping bitterly, and he asked the reason. "Alas! I remember," she replied, "how the full moon was shining as it is now, when I played that air upon a flute and the head of my beloved rose above the water."

The Shepherd looked at her as she spoke with an earnest gaze, and as if a cloud had been taken away from his eyes, he recognised his dear Wife. At the same instant she remembered him, for the moon showed his face clearly; and I am sure no one needs to ask how happy they were, and how happy they remained.

THE SEA-MAIDEN

This twentieth-century Welsh folk-tale was recorded by Stephen Jones and B. L. K. Henderson in their collection *Wonder Tales of Ancient Wales*. As with every story included in this volume, it features a magical creature of the water, but you may also notice another common thread between this and a number of the other stories collected here – from the Scottish selkie to the Māori Pania – specifically, the encounter between a young mortal man and a beautiful woman of the sea by the shore. Despite these similarities, however, each remains strikingly unique, and this story of the Welsh sea maiden is one that comes with some thoroughly unexpected twists and turns. It is also one that perfectly encapsulates the tumultuous relationship we humans have long had with the sea, and why perhaps we've spent so long telling stories of what it holds.

Every day in the week, on Sundays and Holy-days as well as workadays, Ifan Morgan would be down by the sea feasting his eyes on the dancing, glancing waves. Before the first trembling light began to turn the eastern sky a pearly grey, and before the bush-birds gave their first sleepy tweet-tweet, Ifan was wending his way to the waves. Nor was this strange, for Ifan's forefathers had done the same thing; and, in his childhood, he had seen his father fishing in the sea, or watching from the shore. And so Ifan Morgan was like his forefathers. Sometimes in the season he went to catch the frisky mackerel, or the silver herring when it came in shoals near the coast. But his chief delight was to walk along the sea-shore and see what good things his uncle Dafy Jones would bring him; for that was the name by which the Morgans called the great wide sea.

One morning, just as the first pale blue of the dawn stole out of the night, Ifan sat by the great yawning mouths of the dark caves that lay under the hill-sides. His eyes seemed busy searching for

something that could not be found, and, ever and anon, they wandered towards, and dwelt upon the cave of Deio. Fishermen whispered strange and wonderful things about this cave; and there it stood, grim and stark, in the wreathing mists of the morning, a dark patch open to the curling sea. One of Ifan's ancestors had had strange commerce in this cave; and people wondered as to what manner of things happened in its murky depths. Some said that old Deio used to deal there with folk he should not have met, for he carried with him gifts of gold and silver from somewhere; but no one knew whence. The story went on to say that Deio had for his wife, in that dark abode, a sea-maiden. That must be clear for anyone to guess. Otherwise there was no reason for his disappearance for weeks at a time, and his possession of these gifts. But although fishermen often went to seek him they could never trace his whereabouts.

And by this cave sat our friend Ifan, for the times were hard, and a great desire had come upon him to enter the gloomy portals. For more than two years no wreck had come upon that coast. The outlook was very sad for the coming winter, and the mackerel and herring seemed to shun the shore. Up stood Ifan, and, with his mind all of a tremble, he drew near to the mouth—that darksome, open

mouth! And then he came away! Again he approached, wondering if he dared. The tide was running out, he was a good swimmer, and yet he could not enter.

"If the sea-maiden came to me," he said, as he sat down once more, "if she came, I should run for my life. And what would be the good of that? Nothing whatever. I must clutch her, and beg her to marry me, or else I shall get no money. If I married her, then I should have wealth and all the money I could want, and that would be something worth having." Ifan scratched his head, and looked deep into the dark depths.

As he gazed, his eyes saw farther into the darkness and they caught sight of a candle that shed a pale, green light upon a narrow strip of sand which lay along a pool. By this pool sat a young girl combing her hair. Never had Ifan seen aught so lovely. Her fair skin was soft and shimmered like satin, and hair fell in silky, golden showers around her knees. Ifan went slowly towards her, and, as he approached, he heard her weeping bitterly and sighing sorely, while the glittering tears dropped from her eyelids like spring rain-drops sparkling from the sky. He put out his great rough hand and gently stroked her soft, yielding hair in order to check her sorrow. Then he dared to touch her

hand, but she uttered a scream like a savage thing caught in a net, and in spite of all his efforts to calm her, she grew more and more wild and timorous.

Ifan knew not what to do. That he was fortunate to be by the side of such a young and wealthy maiden he felt certain. But how could he win her consent to marriage so that he might get gold and silver wealth? In her hand she held her golden comb, and around her fair neck hung a chain of gleaming pearls. Ifan's heart failed him; all he could do was to pat her hair as though she were one of his brother's children, that her fear might depart. At last he tried again to hold her white hand; but, thereupon, she screamed like half-a-dozen young screech owls, and Ifan heard afar off an answering cry.

"Go away," she cried; "my brother is coming. Hasten! but come to-morrow."

Then there leaped upon Ifan a spray which blinded him, and the pale flame of the green candle went out. Hither and thither was Ifan flung in the waters of the cavern. A rope passed over his head, and he bethought him to utter "Our Father," but there was no time amid the strife. Then in the twinkling of an eye, he was drawn without the cave, and though its sides were sharp with jutting rocks,

and great blue stones lay under the surface of the water, yet he had no harm. The rope was still about him and lay around his waist, and, although he feared to touch it, he longed to draw it to him, for it would make a splendid cable for his boat. In spite of fear he dragged it from the sea. Lo! at its other end he saw fastened a large trunk. He pulled eagerly, and, despite its heavy weight, still he tugged more strongly. But before he could pull it in to the beach, behold, a mighty wave swelled up in the sea and dragged him out of his depth; then once again the sea leaped up, and a wave with a snowy crest lifted him on its bosom, and he found that he stood by the side of the trunk, upon a grassy mound, near the shore.

Who can tell of Ifan's joy when he saw the treasure nestling in the heart of that trunk? Rings set with sparkling gems; chains that glittered like the falling waters when they are scattered from the rock in the sunshine; pearls as white as snow, and rubies red as fire—treasures without price lay before his wondering eyes. He hid them in haste, and, by night, he crept backwards and forwards till all was safe and sound in his cottage home. Then he went to bed and slept.

While yet a few pale stars twinkled faintly in the roseate sky, Ifan walked with a wondering mind

towards the cave of Deio. Far he wandered in the faint and misty light, and ever his thought left him no peace. He wished now he had brought a torch to lighten the darkness of his mystic cave. Now he trembled lest the treasure were the subtle creation of a dream woven in the sleep of the night. Long he waited in the cavern; but no one came, and at last he made his way homeward, feeling that all was not real, and he had but dreamed a dream. Yet at home there lay the wondrous heap of jewels in their settings, so he placed them in skilful array in many a cunning corner, and, when the night had come, he sank again to sleep.

Then, in the darkness, a form came nigh unto him, and damp arms wrapped themselves around him. The more he strove to free himself, the closer grew the embrace, and he heard a whisper, faint as the breath of evening, speak the words, "Forget not to be early in the morn!" "Stay!" cried Ifan. "Wait till I get a light, and I will rise immediately." But before the words had left his lips the visitor had gone; there was nothing. Ifan, rising in haste searched for his treasure, and he saw it by the candle light, gleaming and glittering, gold and silver, gems and pearls, charms and jewels without number.

Again the sun stole silently through the curtain

of the heavens, and Ifan set out for the shore, while fear possessed him as he wandered by the silvery sea. Yes, indeed, fear that never more would his eyes look upon the little white house with thatched roof, the home of his birth and childhood. Then again his heart beat, and he saw in his mind a vision of comfort and welfare. As he mused he stood among his comrades by the sea while they pulled their nets to the shore. It was terrible to hear their language when the nets came home; for not a fish lay within the meshes, and one man cried, "That curse of a sea-maiden has opened our nets and set free the fish."

Ifan stole stealthily away, and then sped along the shore. When he reached Deio's cave, whom should he see at the entrance but the maiden sleeking her hair with a golden comb. Yet to him marvellous was the change which transformed her. Before, she was but a slim girl; now she stood dressed richly like some great lady, and wearing upon her head a crown of purest gold. As Ifan approached she held out her fair hand, saying:

"Comest thou, Ifan? I wish to dwell awhile among the people of the land. Keep this," quoth she, handing him a magic cap, " and I will wear a crown, for I am a king's daughter."

Ifan bent low before her, overcome by her

wondrous beauty, and marvelling that she could be the same.

While yet the mists trembled in the embrace of the morning they two went their way, and Ifan was without speech, for he knew not what to say. He feared to mention his humble home, but even as this thought trod the pathways of his brain she knew of its existence. Turning to him, with a smile like the tender light which steals through the ivy into a darkened room, she said with a ripple of laughter in her voice:

"I know quite well that thou knowest not how to tell me of thy home. But think not of that, for I have long known thee, and seen thee oft, ever since, as a young lad with rosy cheek, thou didst fish from thy father's boat in the bay. In those days, I heard thee sing a song which won for thee the love of my heart. When I spake of thy song and sought to sing it to my father in his palace, all wondered at its music, and wished to hear it from end to end. So I came back often and listened for it, but in vain. Then was I permitted by those who love me to come seeking for thee with treasures, seeking that soul-melody which will not be taught save by treasure. Yet when I met thee I knew that wealth alone would not avail to win thee, but that I must appear as now thou seest me. My name is

Nefyn and I am the daughter to Nefydd-Naf-Neifion. Nor am I without relations in thy world. Think then no more of thy cottage, but do as thou dost desire, and all shall be well."

Then Ifan asked her timidly if she would be his bride, and dwell with him for better or for worse? She answered that she was fain to do so, if he would teach her his song, nor let her see the mystic cap. Then as the day grew brighter so more radiant seemed the face of his affianced bride, while Ifan's song came to him again, and he sang it to Nefyn:

> "Oh, feathered friend with pure blue wing,
> Mild and obedient as a dove,
> Now speed thee, speed thee to the maid
> Who captured all my youthful love.
> Yea, hasten, bird, and tell my sweet,
> Tears stain my face,
> They never tire.
> For her embrace
> I burn with fire—
> Love lingers in my very pace.
> Ah! Beauty slaying me with love—
> May God be gracious to such grace!"

Yet their marriage was not easy, for the news spread abroad that Nefyn was a sea-maiden, and it

was only by their wealth that all was settled. Then indeed they dwelt together in happiness, wandering hand in hand by the sea-shore, and often entering thus into the cave.

Time sped by and Ifan and Nefyn were as nobles in the land. Never was wife more tender and full of grace, nor husband more loving. There were born to them three sons and three daughters, and these children were beauteous as the young and slender flowers that grow in the meadows in the spring time.

One fine day when the sunlight dwelt upon the ocean and its rays were so strong that the young fish could be seen passing to and fro in the crystal depths, Ifan and Nefyn and their children went over the sea in a boat. Suddenly a storm sprang from the sky and the huge waves leapt to meet it. Through the tumult of air and water, screams and cries could be heard, and the children were sorely affrighted. Seeing their terror Nefyn bent over the side of the boat, and her moving lips showed that she was speaking to some one in the depths beneath. Great was the awe of the children at this, and they remembered the rumours that surrounded their mother's origin. Then Nefydd, the eldest son, thought of all he had heard from his parents of Nefydd-Naf-Neifion, and the valleys of

Gwenhidiw, and the country of Gwyn ab Nudd (whose prince came to visit them) and his heart sank, for to him his mother was beautiful beyond compare, tenderest and kindest of all the world. Could she indeed be a sea-maiden from the unknown and mystic depths of the great grey sea?

One day there rode up to the home of Ifan a messenger, and, at night, when the crescent moon was sharp, pointed and pale in the western sky, Ifan and Nefyn departed, leaving the children in charge of a trusted servant. Then Nefydd, who watched them go, said to Eilonwy, his sister, "Why should they set out by night?" So they followed them along the shore. And lo! a huge wave rose from out the glassy sea, and Nefyn, wrapping Ifan and herself in a cloak of skin, sank into the water's heart and passed from sight. At the sad knowledge of his mother's secret, the heart of Nefydd broke within him, and his sister, seeing that her brother was dead, no more desired to live, and flung herself into the sea.

As Eilonwy fell into the waves, a knight of beauteous form, and riding on a snow-white horse, came galloping swiftly over the waves, and bending low from the saddle caught the maiden in his arms, and bore her swiftly away.

In the house of Ifan all was confusion. Nefydd

was dead, Eilonwy had cast herself away and could not be found. What could be done? Then spake Tegid, the brave, handsome brother:

"If we get no message ere the morrow we must bury Nefydd in the waves, and perchance some of my mother's kinsfolk will come and fetch him."

But at midnight a knight came to the house and bade them bury their brother as the early grey dawn crept over the sea.

"Yet," said he, "do not mourn for Nefydd. He shall come back to you and dwell with you once more. And Eilonwy, the fair, lives as the bride of the brightest and bravest knight of Gwerddonau-Llion."

At dawn, they bore the coffin out to sea, and lo! as it sank into the cold waves, those who watched saw Nefydd leave its shelter, and, with his arm around the self-same messenger who bade them hope, he passed into a ship which flew away with them. Then, of a truth, wonder reigned all over the land as to what would happen thereafter.

Time sped by, and, when a year and a day had passed, Ifan, royal in aspect and decked in regal robes, came to his home. Nefyn did not return, for she dwelt with her daughter for a time. All was joy in the homestead, yet in the midst of the joy came the dark stab of sorrow, for Ifan, in the night which

followed, sank into a death slumber, and could not be awakened. Rumour told of a black warrior, who, in the night, stole silently to the house, and as silently departed.

On the morning of Ifan's burial Nefyn returned to the sad home. Bitterly she wept, and in a brief space she left the house again, and Tegid remained as lord. Verily his lot was sad, and he needed all his courage to face the dark looks of his neighbours. So threatening did they become that he sent his sisters away to be educated elsewhere, and he and his brother remained to face the tumult.

One night the brothers dreamed the same dream. They saw, as it were, the black knight pass into Deio's cave. In the morning they went in haste to see if it were so, and before their very eyes the ship which brought their sisters home again was cast upon the rocky shore, and shattered. Yet they hastened to the cave, and here to their horror they beheld the gleaming coils of a huge serpent. As Tegid lifted his sword to strike, the serpent cried aloud:

"Strike me not, Tegid, for I am thy sister imprisoned by the black knight."

As she spoke the black knight came from a deep recess, and whirling his sword aloft struck off the serpent's head. But in vain. Another head came in

its place, and, as it did so, a knight clad in white armour strode from another part. Then the sound of shrewd and awful blows resounded in Deio's cave. Full soon, however, the black knight lay dead in the dark cavern, and, as he died, Eilonwy sprang from the serpent's slough, and Nefyn rose from the waves and bore her children to their father's court—all, that is, except Tegid. He, loving his father dearly, remained for a year and a day by Ifan's grave, often consoled by Nefyn, who came to visit him. Great was his gladness when one day to the faithful lad came Ifan himself. After a long, fond embrace, Tegid, leaning on his loving father's arm, went joyfully to meet his kinsfolk at the Court of Nefydd.

THE MERMAID AND THE BOY

The following tale belongs to the Sámi – the indigenous people of Sápmi, a region that is today encompassed by parts of Russia, Norway, Sweden and Finland. Originally recorded by Jens Andreas Friis in the nineteenth century under the title 'Bardne, Havfruva ja Riddaræva', this translated version was recorded by twentieth century folklorist Andrew Lang in *The Brown Fairy Book* – one of a series of fairy tale collections named after different colours, which bring together stories from around the world. In contrast with the popular image of a daughter bargained away to a witch, like Rapunzel or Sleeping Beauty, who is subsequently saved by a dashing a young prince, 'The Mermaid and the Boy' sees a son promised to a mermaid by his father in exchange for safe passage across the sea. So, who will save him? Surely not a princess . . .

Long, long ago, there lived a king who ruled over a country by the sea. When he had been married about a year, some of his subjects, inhabiting a distant group of islands, revolted against his laws, and it became needful for him to leave his wife and go in person to settle their disputes. The queen feared that some ill would come of it, and implored him to stay at home, but he told her that nobody could do his work for him, and the next morning the sails were spread, and the king started on his voyage.

The vessel had not gone very far when she ran upon a rock, and stuck so fast in a cleft that the strength of the whole crew could not get her off again. To make matters worse, the wind was rising too, and it was quite plain that in a few hours the ship would be dashed to pieces and everybody would be drowned, when suddenly the form of a mermaid was seen dancing on the waves which threatened every moment to overwhelm them.

'There is only one way to free yourselves,' she

said to the king, bobbing up and down in the water as she spoke, 'and that is to give me your solemn word that you will deliver to me the first child that is born to you.'

The king hesitated at this proposal. He hoped that some day he might have children in his home, and the thought that he must yield up the heir to his crown was very bitter to him; but just then a huge wave broke with great force on the ship's side, and his men fell on their knees and entreated him to save them.

So he promised, and this time a wave lifted the vessel clean off the rocks, and she was in the open sea once more.

The affairs of the islands took longer to settle than the king had expected, and some months passed away before he returned to his palace. In his absence a son had been born to him, and so great was his joy that he quite forgot the mermaid and the price he had paid for the safety of his ship. But as the years went on, and the baby grew into a fine big boy, the remembrance of it came back, and one day he told the queen the whole story. From that moment the happiness of both their lives was ruined. Every night they went to bed wondering if they should find his room empty in the morning, and every day they kept him by their

sides, expecting him to be snatched away before their very eyes.

At last the king felt that this state of things could not continue, and he said to his wife:

'After all, the most foolish thing in the world one can do is to keep the boy here in exactly the place in which the mermaid will seek him. Let us give him food and send him on his travels, and perhaps, if the mermaid ever does come to seek him, she may be content with some other child.' And the queen agreed that his plan seemed the wisest.

So the boy was called, and his father told him the story of the voyage, as he had told his mother before him. The prince listened eagerly, and was delighted to think that he was to go away all by himself to see the world, and was not in the least frightened: for though he was now sixteen, he had scarcely been allowed to walk alone beyond the palace gardens. He began busily to make his preparations, and took off his smart velvet coat, putting on instead one of green cloth, while he refused a beautiful bag which the queen offered him to hold his food, and slung a leather knapsack over his shoulders instead, just as he had seen other travellers do. Then he bade farewell to his parents and went his way.

All through the day he walked, watching with

interest the strange birds and animals that darted across his path in the forest or peeped at him from behind a bush. But as evening drew on he became tired, and looked about as he walked for some place where he could sleep. At length he reached a soft mossy bank under a tree, and was just about to stretch himself out on it, when a fearful roar made him start and tremble all over. In another moment something passed swiftly through the air and a lion stood before him.

'What are you doing here?' asked the lion, his eyes glaring fiercely at the boy.

'I am flying from the mermaid,' the prince answered, in a quaking voice.

'Give me some food then,' said the lion, 'it is past my supper time, and I am very hungry.'

The boy was so thankful that the lion did not want to eat *him*, that he gladly picked up his knapsack which lay on the ground, and held out some bread and a flask of wine.

'I feel better now,' said the lion when he had done, 'so I shall go to sleep on this nice soft moss, and if you like you can lie down beside me.' So the boy and the lion slept soundly side by side, till the sun rose.

'I must be off now', remarked the lion, shaking the boy as he spoke; 'but cut off the tip of my

ear, and keep it carefully, and if you are in any danger just wish yourself a lion and you will become one on the spot. One good turn deserves another, you know?'

The prince thanked him for his kindness, and did as he was bid, and the two then bade each other farewell.

'I wonder how it feels to be a lion,' thought the boy, after he had gone a little way; and he took out the tip of the ear from the breast of his jacket and wished with all his might. In an instant his head had swollen to several times its usual size, and his neck seemed very hot and heavy; and, somehow, his hands became paws, and his skin grew hairy and yellow. But what pleased him most was his long tail with a tuft at the end, which he lashed and switched proudly. 'I like being a lion very much,' he said to himself, and trotted gaily along the road.

After a while, however, he got tired of walking in this unaccustomed way—it made his back ache and his front paws felt sore. So he wished himself a boy again, and in the twinkling of an eye his tail disappeared and his head shrank, and the long thick mane became short and curly. Then he looked out for a sleeping place, and found some dry ferns, which he gathered and heaped up.

But before he had time to close his eyes there was a great noise in the trees near by, as if a big heavy body was crashing through them. The boy rose and turned his head, and saw a huge black bear coming towards him.

'What are you doing here?' cried the bear.

'I am running away from the mermaid,' answered the boy; but the bear took no interest in the mermaid, and only said: 'I am hungry; give me something to eat.'

The knapsack was lying on the ground among the fern, but the prince picked it up, and, unfastening the strap, took out his second flask of wine and another loaf of bread. 'We will have supper together;' he remarked politely; but the bear, who had never been taught manners, made no reply, and ate as fast as he could. When he had quite finished, he got up and stretched himself.

'You have got a comfortable-looking bed there,' he observed. 'I really think that, bad sleeper as I am, I might have a good night on it. I can manage to squeeze you in,' he added; 'you don't take up a great deal of room.' The boy was rather indignant at the bear's cool way of talking; but as he was too tired to gather more fern, they lay down side by side, and never stirred till sunrise next morning.

'I must go now,' said the bear, pulling the sleepy

prince on to his feet; 'but first you shall cut off the tip of my ear, and when you are in any danger just wish yourself a bear and you will become one. One good turn deserves another, you know.' And the boy did as he was bid, and he and the bear bade each other farewell.

'I wonder how it feels to be a bear,' thought he to himself when he had walked a little way; and he took out the tip from the breast of his coat and wished hard that he might become a bear. The next moment his body stretched out and thick black fur covered him all over. As before, his hands were changed into paws, but when he tried to switch his tail he found to his disgust that it would not go any distance. 'Why it is hardly worth calling a tail!' said he. For the rest of the day he remained a bear and continued his journey, but as evening came on the bear-skin, which had been so useful when plunging through brambles in the forest, felt rather heavy, and he wished himself a boy again. He was too much exhausted to take the trouble of cutting any fern or seeking for moss, but just threw himself down under a tree, when exactly above his head he heard a great buzzing as a bumble-bee alighted on a honeysuckle branch. 'What are you doing here?' asked the bee in a cross voice; 'at your age you ought to be safe at home.'

'I am running away from the mermaid,' replied the boy; but the bee, like the lion and the bear, was one of those people who never listen to the answers to their questions; and only said: 'I am hungry. Give me something to eat.'

The boy took his last loaf and flask out of his knapsack and laid them on the ground, and they had supper together. 'Well, now I am going to sleep,' observed the bee when the last crumb was gone, 'but as you are not very big I can make room for you beside me,' and he curled up his wings, and tucked in his legs, and he and the prince both slept soundly till morning. Then the bee got up and carefully brushed every scrap of dust off his velvet coat and buzzed loudly in the boy's ear to waken him.

'Take a single hair from one of my wings,' said he, 'and if you are in danger just wish yourself a bee and you will become one. One good turn deserves another, so farewell, and thank you for your supper.' And the bee departed after the boy had pulled out the hair and wrapped it carefully in a leaf.

'It must feel quite different to be a bee from what it does to be a lion or bear,' thought the boy to himself when he had walked for an hour or two. 'I dare say I should get on a great deal faster,' so he pulled out his hair and wished himself a bee.

In a moment the strangest thing happened to him. All his limbs seemed to draw together, and his body to become very short and round; his head grew quite tiny, and instead of his white skin he was covered with the richest, softest velvet. Better than all, he had two lovely gauze wings which carried him the whole day without getting tired.

Late in the afternoon the boy fancied he saw a vast heap of stones a long way off, and he flew straight towards it. But when he reached the gates he saw that it was really a great town, so he wished himself back in his own shape and entered the city.

He found the palace doors wide open and went boldly into a sort of hall which was full of people, and where men and maids were gossiping together. He joined their talk and soon learned from them that the king had only one daughter who had such a hatred to men that she would never suffer one to enter her presence. Her father was in despair, and had had pictures painted of the handsomest princes of all the courts in the world, in the hope that she might fall in love with one of them; but it was no use; the princess would not even allow the pictures to be brought into her room.

'It is late,' remarked one of the women at last; 'I must go to my mistress.' And, turning to one of the lackeys, she bade him find a bed for the youth.

'It is not necessary,' answered the prince, 'this bench is good enough for me. I am used to nothing better.' And when the hall was empty he lay down for a few minutes. But as soon as everything was quiet in the palace he took out the hair and wished himself a bee, and in this shape he flew upstairs, past the guards, and through the keyhole into the princess's chamber. Then he turned himself into a man again.

At this dreadful sight the princess, who was broad awake, began to scream loudly. 'A man! a man!' cried she; but when the guards rushed in there was only a bumble-bee buzzing about the room. They looked under the bed, and behind the curtains, and into the cupboards, then came to the conclusion that the princess had had a bad dream, and bowed themselves out. The door had scarcely closed on them than the bee disappeared, and a handsome youth stood in his place.

'I *knew* a man was hidden somewhere,' cried the princess, and screamed more loudly than before. Her shrieks brought back the guards, but though they looked in all kinds of impossible places no man was to be seen, and so they told the princess.

'He was here a moment ago—I saw him with my own eyes,' and the guards dared not contradict her, though they shook their heads and whispered

to each other that the princess had gone mad on this subject, and saw a man in every table and chair. And they made up their minds that—let her scream as loudly as she might—they would take no notice.

Now the princess saw clearly what they were thinking, and that in future her guards would give her no help, and would perhaps, besides, tell some stories about her to the king, who would shut her up in a lonely tower and prevent her walking in the gardens among her birds and flowers. So when, for the third time, she beheld the prince standing before her, she did not scream but sat up in bed gazing at him in silent terror.

'Do not be afraid,' he said, 'I shall not hurt you'; and he began to praise her gardens, of which he had heard the servants speak, and the birds and flowers which she loved, till the princess's anger softened, and she answered him with gentle words. Indeed, they soon became so friendly that she vowed she would marry no one else, and confided to him that in three days her father would be off to the wars, leaving his sword in her room. If any man could find it and bring it to him he would receive her hand as a reward. At this point a cock crew, and the youth jumped up hastily, saying: 'Of course I shall ride with the king to the war, and if I do not

return, take your violin every evening to the seashore and play on it, so that the very sea-kobolds who live at the bottom of the ocean may hear it and come to you.'

Just as the princess had foretold, in three days the king set out for the war with a large following, and among them was the young prince, who had presented himself at court as a young noble in search of adventures. They had left the city many miles behind them, when the king suddenly discovered that he had forgotten his sword, and though all his attendants instantly offered theirs, he declared that he could fight with none but his own.

'The first man who brings it to me from my daughter's room,' cried he, 'shall not only have her to wife, but after my death shall reign in my stead.'

At this the Red Knight, the young prince, and several more turned their horses to ride as fast as the wind back to the palace. But suddenly a better plan entered the prince's head, and, letting the others pass him, he took his precious parcel from his breast and wished himself a lion. Then on he bounded, uttering such dreadful roars that the horses were frightened and grew unmanageable, and he easily outstripped them, and soon reached

the gates of the palace. Here he hastily changed himself into a bee, and flew straight into the princess's room, where he became a man again. She showed him where the sword hung concealed behind a curtain, and he took it down, saying as he did so: 'Be sure not to forget what you have promised to do.'

The princess made no reply, but smiled sweetly, and slipping a golden ring from her finger she broke it in two and held half out silently to the prince, while the other half she put in her own pocket. He kissed it, and ran down the stairs bearing the sword with him. Some way off he met the Red Knight and the rest, and the Red Knight at first tried to take the sword from him by force. But as the youth proved too strong for him, he gave it up, and resolved to wait for a better opportunity.

This soon came, for the day was hot and the prince was thirsty. Perceiving a little stream that ran into the sea, he turned aside, and, unbuckling the sword, flung himself on the ground for a long drink. Unluckily, the mermaid happened at that moment to be floating on the water not very far off, and knew he was the boy who had been given her before he was born. So she floated gently in to where he was lying, she seized him by the arm, and the waves closed over them both. Hardly had they

disappeared, when the Red Knight stole cautiously up, and could hardly believe his eyes when he saw the king's sword on the bank. He wondered what had become of the youth, who an hour before had guarded his treasure so fiercely; but, after all, that was no affair of his! So, fastening the sword to his belt, he carried it to the king.

The war was soon over, and the king returned to his people, who welcomed him with shouts of joy. But when the princess from her window saw that her betrothed was not among the attendants riding behind her father, her heart sank, for she knew that some evil must have befallen him, and she feared the Red Knight. She had long ago learned how clever and how wicked he was, and something whispered to her that it was *he* who would gain the credit of having carried back the sword, and would claim her as his bride, though he had never even entered her chamber. And she could do nothing; for although the king loved her, he never let her stand in the way of his plans.

The poor princess was only too right, and everything came to pass exactly as she had foreseen it. The king told her that the Red Knight had won her fairly, and that the wedding would take place next day, and there would be a great feast after it.

In those days feasts were much longer and more splendid than they are now; and it was growing dark when the princess, tired out with all she had gone through, stole up to her own room for a little quiet. But the moon was shining so brightly over the sea that it seemed to draw her towards it, and taking her violin under her arm, she crept down to the shore.

'Listen! listen!' said the mermaid to the prince, who was lying stretched on a bed of seaweeds at the bottom of the sea. 'Listen! that is your old love playing, for mermaids know everything that happens upon earth.'

'I hear nothing,' answered the youth, who did not look happy. 'Take me up higher, where the sounds can reach me'.

So the mermaid took him on her shoulders and bore him up midway to the surface. 'Can you hear now?' she asked.

'No,' answered the prince, 'I hear nothing but the water rushing; I must go higher still.'

Then the mermaid carried him to the very top. 'You must surely be able to hear *now*?' said she.

'Nothing but the water,' repeated the youth. So she took him right to the land.

'At any rate you can hear *now*?' she said again.

'The water is still rushing in my ears,' answered

he; 'but wait a little, that will soon pass off.' And as he spoke he put his hand into his breast, and seizing the hair wished himself a bee, and flew straight into the pocket of the princess. The mermaid looked in vain for him, and floated all night upon the sea; but he never came back, and never more did he gladden her eyes. But the princess felt that something strange was about her, though she knew not what, and returned quickly to the palace, where the young man at once resumed his own shape. Oh, what joy filled her heart at the sight of him! But there was no time to be lost, and she led him right into the hall, where the king and his nobles were still sitting at the feast. 'Here is a man who boasts that he can do wonderful tricks,' said she, 'better even than the Red Knight's! That cannot be true, of course; but it might be well to give this impostor a lesson. He pretends, for instance, that he can turn himself into a lion; but that I do not believe. I know that you have studied the art of magic,' she went on, turning to the Red Knight, 'so suppose you just show him how it is done, and bring shame upon him.'

Now the Red Knight had never opened a book of magic in his life; but he was accustomed to think that he could do everything better than other people without any teaching at all. So he turned

and twisted himself about, and bellowed and made faces; but he did not become a lion for all that.

'Well, perhaps it *is* very difficult to change into a lion. Make yourself a bear,' said the princess. But the Red Knight found it no easier to become a bear than a lion.

'Try a bee,' suggested she. 'I have always read that anyone who can do magic at all can do that.' And the old knight buzzed and hummed, but he remained a man and not a bee.

'Now it is your turn,' said the princess to the youth. 'Let us see if you can change yourself into a lion.' And in a moment such a fierce creature stood before them, that all the guests rushed out of the hall, treading each other underfoot in their fright. The lion sprang at the Red Knight, and would have torn him in pieces had not the princess held him back, and bidden him to change himself into a man again. And in a second a man took the place of the lion.

'Now become a bear,' said she; and a bear advanced panting and stretching out his arms to the Red Knight, who shrank behind the princess.

By this time some of the guests had regained their courage, and returned as far as the door, thinking that if it was safe for the princess perhaps it was safe for them. The king, who was braver

than they, and felt it needful to set them a good example besides, had never left his seat, and when at a new command of the princess the bear once more turned into a man, he was silent from astonishment, and a suspicion of the truth began to dawn on him. 'Was it *he* who fetched the sword?' asked the king.

'Yes, it was,' answered the princess; and she told him the whole story, and how she had broken her gold ring and given him half of it. And the prince took out his half of the ring, and the princess took out hers, and they fitted exactly. Next day the Red Knight was hanged, as he richly deserved, and there was a new marriage feast for the prince and princess.

THE SHARK MAN

Meet Nanaue: the Hawaiian shark man; a figure whom even if you are not familiar with Polynesian mythology you might recognize as the inspiration behind DC Comics' King Shark. The following story tells the tale of Nanaue's origins as it was recorded by Thomas G. Thrum in his twentieth-century collection *Hawaiian Folk Tales*, based on Mrs E. M. Nakuina's narration. Nanaue, as this story shows, is not the only shark man/god to hail from Hawaii, likely due to the sheer number of sharks that occupy the surrounding waters – forty identifiable species to be exact. While sharks often get an unfairly bad rap (thanks, *Jaws*) there is no denying that certain species pose a risk to those who venture out to sea – it comes as no surprise that in a collection of stories highlighting humanity's tumultuous relationship with water there should be at least one shark man here.

Kamohoalii, the King-shark of Hawaii and Maui, has several deep sea caves that he uses in turn as his habitat. There are several of these at the bottom of the palisades, extending from Waipio toward Kohala, on the island of Hawaii. A favorite one was at Koamano, on the mainland, and another was at Maiaukiu, the small islet just abreast of the valley of Waipio. It was the belief of the ancient Hawaiians that several of these shark gods could assume any shape they chose, the human form even, when occasion demanded.

In the reign of Umi, a beautiful girl, called Kalei, living in Waipio, was very fond of shellfish, and frequently went to Kuiopihi for her favorite article of diet. She generally went in the company of other women, but if the sea was a little rough, and her usual companion was afraid to venture out on the wild and dangerous beach, she very often went alone rather than go without her favorite seashells.

In those days the Waipio River emptied over a

low fall into a basin partly open to the sea; this basin is now completely filled up with rocks from some convulsion of nature, which has happened since then. In this was a deep pool, a favorite bathing-place for all Waipio. The King shark god, Kamohoalii, used to visit this pool very often to sport in the fresh waters of the Waipio River. Taking into account the many different tales told of the doings of this shark god, he must have had quite an eye for human physical beauty.

Kalei, as was to be expected from a strong, well-formed Hawaiian girl of those days, was an expert swimmer, a good diver, and noted for the neatness and grace with which she would *lelekawa* (jump from the rocks into deep water) without any splashing of water, which would happen to unskilful divers, from the awkward attitudes they would assume in the act of jumping.

It seems Kamohoalii, the King-shark, had noted the charms of the beautiful Kalei, and his heart, or whatever answers in place of it with fishes, had been captured by them. But he could not expect to make much of an impression on the maiden's susceptibilities in *propria persona*, even though he was perfectly able to take her bodily into his capacious maw; so he must needs go courting in a more pleasing way. Assuming the form of a very

handsome man, he walked on the beach one rather rough morning, waiting for the girl's appearance.

Now the very wildness of the elements afforded him the chance he desired, as, though Kalei was counted among the most agile and quick of rock-fishers, that morning, when she did come, and alone, as her usual companions were deterred by the rough weather, she made several unsuccessful springs to escape a high threatening wave raised by the god himself; and apparently, if it had not been for the prompt and effective assistance rendered by the handsome stranger, she would have been swept out into the sea.

Thus an acquaintance was established. Kalei met the stranger from time to time, and finally became his wife.

Some little time before she expected to become a mother, her husband, who all this time would only come home at night, told her his true nature, and informing her that he would have to leave her, gave orders in regard to the bringing up of the future child. He particularly cautioned the mother never to let him be fed on animal flesh of any kind, as he would be born with a dual nature, and with a body that he could change at will.

In time Kalei was delivered of a fine healthy boy, apparently the same as any other child, but he

had, besides the normal mouth of a human being, a shark's mouth on his back between the shoulder blades. Kalei had told her family of the kind of being her husband was, and they all agreed to keep the matter of the shark-mouth on the child's back a secret, as there was no knowing what fears and jealousies might be excited in the minds of the King or high chiefs by such an abnormal being, and the babe might be killed.

The old grandfather, far from heeding the warning given by Kamohoalii in the matter of animal diet, as soon as the boy, who was called Nanaue, was old enough to come under the taboo in regard to the eating of males, and had to take his meals at the mua house with the men of the family, took especial pains to feed him on dog meat and pork. He had a hope that his grandson would grow up to be a great, strong man, and become a famous warrior; and there was no knowing what possibilities lay before a strong, skilful warrior in those days. So he fed the boy with meat, whenever it was obtainable. The boy thrived, grew strong, big, and handsome as a young lama (*Maba sandwicensis*) tree.

There was another pool with a small fall of the Waipio River very near the house of Kalei, and the boy very often went into it while his mother

watched on the banks. Whenever he got into the water he would take the form of a shark and would chase and eat the small fish which abounded in the pool. As he grew old enough to understand, his mother took especial pains to impress on him the necessity of concealing his shark nature from other people.

This place was also another favorite bathing-place of the people, but Nanaue, contrary to all the habits of a genuine Hawaiian, would never go in bathing with the others, but always alone; and when his mother was able, she used to go with him and sit on the banks, holding the kapa scarf, which he always wore to hide the shark-mouth on his back.

When he became a man, his appetite for animal diet, indulged in childhood, had grown so strong that a human being's ordinary allowance would not suffice for him. The old grandfather had died in the meantime, so that he was dependent on the food supplied by his stepfather and uncles, and they had to expostulate with him on what they called his shark-like voracity. This gave rise to the common native nickname of a *manohae* (ravenous shark) for a very gluttonous man, especially in the matter of meat.

Nanaue used to spend a good deal of his time

in the two pools, the one inland and the other opening into the sea. The busy-bodies (they had some in those days as well as now) were set to wondering why he always kept a *kihei*, or mantle, on his shoulders; and for such a handsomely shaped, athletic young man, it was indeed a matter of wonder and speculation, considering the usual attire of the youth of those days. He also kept aloof from all the games and pastimes of the young people, for fear that the wind or some active movement might displace the kapa mantle, and the shark-mouth be exposed to view.

About this time children and eventually grown-up people began to disappear mysteriously.

Nanaue had one good quality that seemed to redeem his apparent unsociability; he was almost always to be seen working in his mother's taro or potato patch when not fishing or bathing. People going to the sea beach would have to pass these potato or taro patches, and it was Nanaue's habit to accost them with the query of where they were going. If they answered, "To bathe in the sea," or, "Fishing," he would answer, "Take care, or you may disappear head and tail." Whenever he so accosted any one it would not be long before some member of the party so addressed would be bitten by a shark.

If it should be a man or woman going to the beach alone, that person would never be seen again, as the shark-man would immediately follow, and watching for a favorable opportunity, jump into the sea. Having previously marked the whereabouts of the person he was after, it was an easy thing for him to approach quite close, and changing into a shark, rush on the unsuspecting person and drag him or her down into the deep, where he would devour his victim at his leisure. This was the danger to humanity which his king-father foresaw when he cautioned the mother of the unborn child about feeding him on animal flesh, as thereby an appetite would be evoked which they had no means of satisfying, and a human being would furnish the most handy meal of the kind that he would desire.

Nanaue had been a man grown some time, when an order was promulgated by Umi, King of Hawaii, for every man dwelling in Waipio to go to *koele* work, tilling a large plantation for the King. There were to be certain days in an *anahulu* (ten days) to be set aside for this work, when every man, woman, and child had to go and render service, excepting the very old and decrepit, and children in arms.

The first day every one went but Nanaue. He

kept on working in his mother's vegetable garden to the astonishment of all who saw him. This was reported to the King, and several stalwart men were sent after him. When brought before the King he still wore his *kapa kihei*, or mantle.

The King asked him why he was not doing koele work with every one else. Nanaue answered he did not know it was required of him. Umi could not help admiring the bold, free bearing of the handsome man, and noting his splendid physique, thought he would make a good warrior, greatly wanted in those ages, and more especially in the reign of Umi, and simply ordered him to go to work.

Nanaue obeyed, and took his place in the field with the others, and proved himself a good worker, but still kept on his kihei, which it would be natural to suppose that he would lay aside as an incumbrance when engaged in hard labor. At last some of the more venturesome of the younger folks managed to tear his kapa off, as if accidentally, when the shark-mouth on his back was seen by all the people near.

Nanaue was so enraged at the displacement of his kapa and his consequent exposure, that he turned and bit several of the crowd, while the shark-mouth opened and shut with a snap, and a

clicking sound was heard such as a shark is supposed to make when baulked by its prey.

The news of the shark-mouth and his characteristic shark-like actions were quickly reported to the King, with the fact of the disappearance of so many people in the vicinity of the pools frequented by Nanaue; and of his pretended warnings to people going to the sea, which were immediately followed by a shark bite or by their being eaten bodily, with every one's surmise and belief that this man was at the bottom of all those disappearances. The King believed it was even so, and ordered a large fire to be lighted, and Nanaue to be thrown in to be burnt alive.

When Nanaue saw what was before him, he called on the shark god, his father, to help him; then, seeming to be endowed with superhuman strength in answer to his prayer, he burst the ropes with which he had been bound in preparation for the burning, and breaking through the throng of Umi's warriors, who attempted to detain him, he ran, followed by the whole multitude, toward the pool that emptied into the sea. When he got to the edge of the rocks bordering the pool, he waited till the foremost persons were within arm's length, when he leaped into the water and immediately turned into a large shark on the surface of the

water, in plain view of the people who had arrived, and whose numbers were being continually augmented by more and more arrivals.

He lay on the surface some little time, as if to recover his breath, and then turned over on his back, and raising his head partly out of the water, snapped his teeth at the crowd who, by this time, completely lined the banks, and then, as if in derision or defiance of them, turned and flirted his tail at them and swam out to sea.

The people and chiefs were for killing his mother and relatives for having brought up such a monster. Kalei and her brothers were seized, bound, and dragged before Umi, while the people clamored for their immediate execution, or as some suggested, that they be thrown into the fire lighted for Nanaue.

But Umi was a wise king and would not consent to any such summary proceedings, but questioned Kalei in regard to her fearful offspring. The grieved and frightened mother told everything in connection with the paternity and bringing up of the child, and with the warning given by the dread sea-father.

Umi considered that the great sea god Kamohoalii was on the whole a beneficent as well as a powerful one. Should the relatives and mother of

that shark god's son be killed, there would then be no possible means of checking the ravages of that son, who might linger around the coast and creeks of the island, taking on human shape at will, for the purpose of travelling inland to any place he liked, and then reassume his fish form and lie in wait in the many deep pools formed by the streams and springs.

Umi, therefore, ordered Kalei and her relatives to be set at liberty, while the priests and shark kahunas were requested to make offerings and invocations to Kamohoalii that his spirit might take possession of one of his *hakas* (mediums devoted to his cult), and so express to humanity his desires in regard to his bad son, who had presumed to eat human beings, a practice well known to be contrary to Kamohoalii's design.

This was done, whereupon the shark god manifested himself through a haka, and expressed his grief at the action of his wayward son. He told them that the grandfather was to blame for feeding him on animal flesh contrary to his orders, and if it were not for that extenuating circumstance, he would order his son to be killed by his own shark officers; but as it was, he would require of him that he should disappear forever from the shores of Hawaii. Should Nanaue disregard that order and

be seen by any of his father's shark soldiers, he was to be instantly killed.

Then the shark god, who it seems retained an affection for his human wife, exacted a promise that she and her relatives were to be forever free from any persecutions on account of her unnatural son, on pain of the return and freedom from the taboo of that son.

Accordingly Nanaue left the island of Hawaii, crossed over to Maui, and landing at Kipahulu, resumed his human shape and went inland. He was seen by the people, and when questioned, told them he was a traveller from Hawaii, who had landed at Hana and was going around sightseeing. He was so good looking, pleasant, and beguiling in his conversation that people generally liked him. He was taken as *aikane* by one of the petty chiefs of the place, who gave his own sister for wife to Nanaue. The latter made a stipulation that his sleeping house should be separated from that of his wife, on account of a pretended vow, but really in order that his peculiar second mouth might escape detection.

For a while the charms of the pretty girl who had become his wife seem to have been sufficient to prevent him from trying to eat human beings, but after a while, when the novelty of his position as a husband had worn off, and the desire for

human flesh had again become very strong, he resumed the old practice for which he had been driven away from Hawaii.

He was eventually detected in the very act of pushing a girl into the sea, jumping in after her, then turning into a shark, and commencing to devour her, to the horror of some people who were fishing with hook and rod from some rocks where he had not observed them. These people raised the alarm, and Nanaue seeing that he was discovered, left for Molokai where he was not known.

He took up his residence on Molokai at Poniuohua, adjoining the ahupuaa of Kainalu, and it was not very long before he was at his old practice of observing and accosting people, giving them his peculiar warning, following them to the sea in his human shape, then seizing one of them as a shark and pulling the unfortunate one to the bottom, where he would devour his victim. In the excitement of such an occurrence, people would fail to notice his absence until he would reappear at some distant point far away from the throng, as if engaged in shrimping or crabbing.

This went on for some time, till the frightened and harassed people in desperation went to consult a shark kahuna, as the ravages of the man-eating shark had put a practical taboo on all kinds of

fishing. It was not safe to be anywhere near the sea, even in the shallowest water.

The kahuna told them to lie in wait for Nanaue, and the next time he prophesied that a person would be eaten head and tail, to have some strong men seize him and pull off his kapa mantle, when a shark mouth would be found on his back. This was done, and the mouth seen, but the shark-man was so strong when they seized him and attempted to bind him, that he broke away from them several times. He was finally overpowered near the seashore and tightly bound. All the people then turned their attention to gathering brush and firewood to burn him, for it was well known that it is only by being totally consumed by fire that a man-shark can be thoroughly destroyed, and prevented from taking possession of the body of some harmless fish shark, who would then be incited to do all the pernicious acts of a man-shark.

While he lay there on the low sandy beach, the tide was coming in, and as most of the people were returning with fagots and brush, Nanaue made a supreme effort and rolled over so that his feet touched the water, when he was enabled at once to change into a monster shark. Those who were near him saw it, but were not disposed to let him off so easily, and they ran several rows of netting makai,

the water being very shallow for quite a distance out. The shark's flippers were all bound by the ropes with which the man Nanaue had been bound, and this with the shallowness of the water prevented him from exerting his great strength to advantage. He did succeed in struggling to the breakers, though momentarily growing weaker from loss of blood, as the people were striking at him with clubs, spears, stone adzes and anything that would hurt or wound, so as to prevent his escape.

With all that, he would have got clear, if the people had not called to their aid the demigod Unauna, who lived in the mountains of upper Kainalu. It was then a case of Akua *vs.* Akua, but Unauna was only a young demigod, and not supposed to have acquired his full strength and supernatural powers, while Nanaue was a full-grown man and shark. If it had not been for the latter's being hampered by the cords with which he was bound, the nets in his way, as well as the loss of blood, it is fully believed that he would have got the better of the young local presiding deity; but he was finally conquered and hauled up on the hill slopes of Kainalu to be burnt.

The shallow ravine left by the passage of his immense body over the light yielding soil of the

Kainalu Hill slope can be seen to this day, as also a ring or deep groove completely around the top of a tall insulated rock very near the top of Kainalu Hill, around which Unauna had thrown the rope, to assist him in hauling the big shark uphill. The place was ever afterwards called Puumano (Shark Hill), and is so known to this day.

Nanaue was so large, that in the attempt to burn him, the blood and water oozing out of his burning body put out the fire several times. Not to be outwitted in that way by the shark son of Kamohoalii, Unauna ordered the people to cut and bring for the purpose of splitting into knives, bamboos from the sacred grove of Kainalu. The shark flesh was then cut into strips, partly dried, and then burnt, but the whole bamboo grove had to be used before the big shark was all cut. The god Mohoalii (another form of the name of the god Kamohoalii), father of Unauna, was so angered by the desecration of the grove, or more likely on account of the use to which it was put, that he took away all the edge and sharpness from the bamboos of this grove forever, and to this day they are different from the bamboos of any other place or grove on the islands, in this particular, that a piece of them cannot cut any more than any piece of common wood.

FLORY CANTILLON'S FUNERAL

'Flory Cantillon's Funeral' is a fascinating story of ancestry, tradition, and our ties to both land and sea. Originally recorded by Thomas Crofton Croker in his nineteenth-century collection *Fairy Legends and Traditions of the South of Ireland*, it takes place off the coast of Ballyheigue, Ireland. It recounts the tale of a man named Connor who, curious about the burial traditions of the family he has married into – whereby they leave their coffins to be swallowed by the sea – sets out to investigate. It is here he spies creatures described only as 'strange' and 'mysterious-looking figures' but who very well could be merrow (murúch) – the Irish equivalent of the mermaid. Either way it reminds us not only of the mystery inherent in the sea but the fine line between its watery depths and a world that might exist beyond death.

The ancient burial-place of the Cantillon family was on an island in Ballyheigh Bay. This island was situated at no great distance from the shore, and at a remote period was overflowed in one of the incroachments which the Atlantic has made on that part of the coast of Kerry. The fishermen declare they have often seen the ruined walls of an old chapel beneath them in the water, as they sailed over the clear green sea, of a sunny afternoon.*
However this may be, it is well known that the Cantillons were, like most other Irish families, strongly attached to their ancient burial-place; and this attachment led to the custom, when any of the family died, of carrying the corpse to the sea-side, where the coffin was left on the shore within reach of the tide. In the morning it had disappeared,

---

* "The neighbouring inhabitants," says Dr. Smith, in his History of Kerry, speaking of Ballyheigh, "show some rocks visible in this bay only at low tides, which, they say, are the remains of an island, that was formerly the burial-place of the family of Cantillon, the ancient proprietors of Ballyheigh." p. 210.

being, as was traditionally believed, conveyed away by the ancestors of the deceased to their family tomb.

Connor Crowe, a county Clare man, was related to the Cantillons by marriage. "Connor Mac in Cruagh, of the seven quarters of Breintragh," as he was commonly called, and a proud man he was of the name. Connor, be it known, would drink a quart of salt water, for its medicinal virtues, before breakfast; and for the same reason, I suppose, double that quantity of raw whiskey between breakfast and night, which last he did with as little inconvenience to himself as any man in the barony of Moyferta; and were I to add Clanderalaw and Ibrickan, I don't think I should say wrong.

On the death of Florence Cantillon, Connor Crowe was determined to satisfy himself about the truth of this story of the old church under the sea: so when he heard the news of the old fellow's death, away with him to Ardfert, where Flory was laid out in high style, and a beautiful corpse he made.

Flory had been as jolly and as rollocking a boy in his day as ever was stretched, and his wake was in every respect worthy of him. There was all kind of entertainment and all sort of diversion at it, and no less than three girls got husbands there—more luck to them. Every thing was as it should be: all that side of the country, from Dingle to Tarbert,

was at the funeral. The Keen was sung long and bitterly; and, according to the family custom, the coffin was carried to Ballyheigh strand, where it was laid upon the shore with a prayer for the repose of the dead.

The mourners departed, one group after another, and at last Connor Crowe was left alone: he then pulled out his whiskey bottle, his drop of comfort as he called it, which he required, being in grief; and down he sat upon a big stone that was sheltered by a projecting rock, and partly concealed from view, to await with patience the appearance of the ghostly undertakers.

The evening came on mild and beautiful; he whistled an old air which he had heard in his childhood, hoping to keep idle fears out of his head; but the wild strain of that melody brought a thousand recollections with it, which only made the twilight appear more pensive.

"If 't was near the gloomy tower of Dunmore, in my own sweet county, I was," said Connor Crowe, with a sigh, "one might well believe that the prisoners, who were murdered long ago, there in the vaults under the castle, would be the hands to carry off the coffin out of envy, for never a one of them was buried decently, nor had as much as a coffin amongst them all. 'Tis often, sure enough,

I have heard lamentations and great mourning coming from the vaults of Dunmore Castle; but," continued he, after fondly pressing his lips to the mouth of his companion and silent comforter, the whiskey bottle, "didn't I know all the time well enough, 't was the dismal sounding waves working through the cliffs and hollows of the rocks, and fretting themselves to foam. Oh then, Dunmore Castle, it is you that are the gloomy looking tower on a gloomy day, with the gloomy hills behind you; when one has gloomy thoughts on their heart, and sees you like a ghost rising out of the smoke made by the kelp burners on the strand, there is, the Lord save us! as fearful a look about you as about the Blue Man's Lake at midnight. Well then, any how," said Connor, after a pause, "is it not a blessed night, though surely the moon looks mighty pale in the face? St. Senan himself between us and all kinds of harm."

It was, in truth, a lovely moonlight night; nothing was to be seen around but the dark rocks, and the white pebbly beach, upon which the sea broke with a hoarse and melancholy murmur. Connor, notwithstanding his frequent draughts, felt rather queerish, and almost began to repent his curiosity. It was certainly a solemn sight to behold the black coffin resting upon the white strand. His

imagination gradually converted the deep moaning of old ocean into a mournful wail for the dead, and from the shadowy recesses of the rocks he imaged forth strange and visionary forms.

As the night advanced, Connor became weary with watching; he caught himself more than once in the fact of nodding, when suddenly giving his head a shake, he would look towards the black coffin. But the narrow house of death remained unmoved before him.

It was long past midnight, and the moon was sinking into the sea, when he heard the sound of many voices, which gradually became stronger, above the heavy and monotonous roll of the sea: he listened, and presently could distinguish a Keen, of exquisite sweetness, the notes of which rose and fell with the heaving of the waves, whose deep murmur mingled with and supported the strain!

The Keen grew louder and louder, and seemed to approach the beach, and then fell into a low plaintive wail. As it ended, Connor beheld a number of strange, and in the dim light, mysterious-looking figures, emerge from the sea, and surround the coffin, which they prepared to launch into the water.

"This comes of marrying with the creatures

of earth," said one of the figures, in a clear, yet hollow tone.

"True," replied another, with a voice still more fearful, "our king would never have commanded his gnawing white-toothed waves to devour the rocky roots of the island cemetery, had not his daughter, Durfulla, been buried there by her mortal husband!"

"But the time will come," said a third, bending over the coffin.

"When mortal eye—our work shall spy.

And mortal ear—our dirge shall hear."

"Then," said a fourth, "our burial of the Cantillons is at an end for ever!"

As this was spoken, the coffin was borne from the beach by a retiring wave, and the company of sea people prepared to follow it: but at the moment, one chanced to discover Connor Crowe, as fixed with wonder and as motionless with fear as the stone on which he sat.

"The time is come," cried the unearthly being, "the time is come; a human eye looks on the forms of ocean, a human ear has heard their voices; farewell to the Cantillons; the sons of the sea are no longer doomed to bury the dust of the earth!"

One after the other turned slowly round, and regarded Connor Crowe, who still remained as if

bound by a spell. Again arose their funeral song; and on the next wave they followed the coffin. The sound of the lamentation died away, and at length nothing was heard but the rush of waters. The coffin and the train of sea people sank over the old church-yard, and never, since the funeral of old Flory Cantillon, have any of the family been carried to the strand of Ballyheigh, for conveyance to their rightful burial-place, beneath the waves of the Atlantic.

THE MERMAID

The following tale has been taken from the second volume of *The Far East*, the English edition of *Kokumin no tomo*, a nineteenth-century journal originally published in Tokyo. It centres on a lonely fisherman and his encounter with – surprise, surprise – a mermaid. In Japanese folklore the mermaid, or the creature most like her, is known as a ningyo or 'human-fish' and according to various tales it is good luck to eat their flesh – something our own protagonist grapples with. Part fish, part human, one notable feature of the ningyo is that they are sometimes depicted as a fish with only the head of a man or woman. This is the case for the original illustration that accompanies the story of 'The Mermaid' in *The Far East*, so it's worth bearing that in mind while you read the following story.

In days of yore, so runs the Japanese legend as interpreted in the *Nihen no Mukashihamashi* (Old Legends of Japan) there lived a man, a good-natured soul, who yearned to be married but had reached middle-age without finding a suitable partner of his joys and sorrows. His joys consisted mainly in fishing with rod and line from the rocks or the river-bank: his sorrows were most acute when he reached home tired at night and found no one to welcome him and to cook the fish that he had hooked.

One day he was sitting, rod in hand, on a rock meditating on his forlorn and solitary condition when suddenly he felt a tug at his line and found that he had hooked something out of the common. Fearing to break his line and lose both tackle and fish he warily played it for some time and at last succeeded in landing it on the rocks, when to his surprise he found that it was no real fish, but a mermaid with the face of a beautiful maiden, and a body which ended in the orthodox tail.

"Desinit in piscem mulier formosa superme." The mermaid's face was tearful, for the hook was in her cheek, and there was also the shame of being forcibly dragged out of her native element; and the angler was a man of tender heart.

Gently extracting the hook from her jaws, he held her in his hands and meditatively speculated on the money which he could gain by selling her to an itinerant exhibition, or the long life which he might obtain by eating her flesh, (it being, according to the Japanese legend, the peculiar property of mermaid's flesh to give perpetual youth and life to those who eat it).

But his soul revolted at the thought of eating this fair creature, that whimpered and cried like a human being, and so after another long gaze he threw it back into the waves, when the mermaid, waving its grateful adieux, speedily dived out of sight.

The man (his name does not appear in the story) then went on with his fishing. He caught an astonishingly large number of fish and at evening returned home satisfied not only on account of his great catch, but also because of the act of kindness which he had performed. That night as he was in his kitchen, with his sleeves tucked up, preparing his supper, he heard a gentle voice, as of a woman,

calling to him from the front of the house. On going to open the door, he found a woman of ordinary appearance but with a sweet and loveable countenance, who told him that she was a homeless and belated traveller who begged a night's lodging.

"Come right in," he said, " and make the best you can of my poor accommodation," Then, showing her into the parlour, be begged her to sit down and rest a little while he got ready the supper, and went off into the kitchen. But the woman followed him, and peering over his shoulder as he was scraping the fish said:

"Won't you let me earn my supper by helping you with the cooking?"

"No, no," replied the man, "it would be poor hospitality to make my guest work in the kitchen. Please go into the parlour and sit down. I'll be with you directly."

But the woman insisted that she had lived all her life by the seaside, that she knew all manner of beautiful recipes for cooking fish, and that it was but right that she should do something for her night's entertainment; and being a woman she got her way.

Never before had such delicious fish been served in that poor bachelor's house. He ate what was set before him and came again for a second

help and a third, and then fell to expressing his regret that he could not hope to have such a supper every night. Then coyly and modestly the lady remarked that such a hope need not be beyond his powers of attainment; and when pressed for an explanation of this speech, she let fall a modest tear and said that she was a lone woman without parents and without a home. He was, as we have before said, a tenderhearted man, and the upshot of it all was that the lady consented to become the mistress of his house, his hand, and his heart.

But on conditions:—when in the first burst of joy, he was about to press his newly found treasure to his heart, "My dear" she said, holding out a warning hand, "My dear, you know I have lived all my life by the sea side, and I can't do without my salt-water bath once a week. Promise me that" He readily assented. "And promise me," she continued, "never to come in, nor to look, while I am taking my bath." It was such a simple request and such a natural one, that the lover (for he was that now) could but joyfully acquiesce and congratulate himself that he had obtained so great a treasure on such easy terms.

So they were married, and lived happily for many months. The fish were always excellently

cooked now, and the husband grew sleek and comfortable, as men do when they have got wives at home who take good care of them. But the bath! It was her one pleasure and diversion, and she took the whole morning preparing for it, and stayed in for hours in the afternoon, and then spent the rest of the day in adorning her person after her bath. So that when bath day came around her husband had a poor time of it. Still he bore it patiently, satisfied with his bargain, till one fatal afternoon when he came home and found her as usual in her bath. The doors were shut, but there was a chink, and he was hungrily anxious to know how long it would be before he got his supper. So he just peeped in to see how long she was going to be, when to his surprise and horror, he saw no wife, but a mermaid swimming about in the bath-tub.

"Ah!" he said, with half a shudder, "now I understand why she is such a good hand at cooking fish. I hope she did not see me peeping at her, but all the same I don't think I shall be able to eat those fish as heartily hereafter."

Presently the door opened and his wife appeared. With a tearful face she knelt down before him and said, "You were kind to me long ago when you saved my life out fishing. In order to

repay your kindness I came to help you and be your cook. You have treated me with unfailing kindness, and have honoured me by making me your wife. I cannot thank you enough for all you have done. But, alas! you have seen me in my true form, and now I can stay with you no longer. It grieves me to the heart, but I must bid you good-bye. Heaven bless you, and give you a long and prosperous life." And before he could speak she was away on the rocks and plunged into the sea.

Poor man! by one thoughtless act he had lost a good wife, and as his marriage with a mermaid had procured for him the gift of a long life, there were many lonely days of widowerhood in store for him.

The fable appears to have two morals. The one is that if a lady wishes to gain and to keep a good husband, she should feed him. The other is that if you wish to retain the affections of a good wife you should not interfere with her toilet.

THE SEAL CATCHER AND THE MERMAN

It is time to return to Scotland where the term mermaid/merman is once again used to refer to the legendary selkie – less fish, more seal – and in this instance a selkie who can take the form of a human man. The tale of 'The Seal Catcher and the Merman' is another which was recorded by the twentieth-century author and folklorist Elizabeth Grierson. While our titular seal catcher has no interest in marriage, there is certainly overlap with his treatment of the seal in question: how can this creature benefit me? The story poses questions of how we should treat others and the world around us, but what those conclusions are I shall I leave to you. I do believe, however, that the selkie/merman in this story would likely be pleased to learn that seals are now a protected species in Scotland.

Once upon a time there was a man who lived not very far from John o' Groat's house, which, as everyone knows, is in the very north of Scotland. He lived in a little cottage by the sea-shore, and made his living by catching seals and selling their fur, which is very valuable.

He earned a good deal of money in this way, for these creatures used to come out of the sea in large numbers, and lie on the rocks near his house basking in the sunshine, so that it was not difficult to creep up behind them and kill them.

Some of those seals were larger than others, and the country people used to call them "Roane," and whisper that they were not seals at all, but Mermen and Merwomen, who came from a country of their own, far down under the ocean, who assumed this strange disguise in order that they might pass through the water, and come up to breathe the air of this earth of ours.

But the seal catcher only laughed at them, and said that those seals were most worth killing, for

their skins were so big that he got an extra price for them.

Now it chanced one day, when he was pursuing his calling, that he stabbed a seal with his hunting-knife, and whether the stroke had not been sure enough or not, I cannot say, but with a loud cry of pain the creature slipped off the rock into the sea, and disappeared under the water, carrying the knife along with it.

The seal catcher, much annoyed at his clumsiness, and also at the loss of his knife, went home to dinner in a very downcast frame of mind. On his way he met a horseman, who was so tall and so strange-looking and who rode on such a gigantic horse, that he stopped and looked at him in astonishment, wondering who he was, and from what country he came.

The stranger stopped also, and asked him his trade and on hearing that he was a seal catcher, he immediately ordered a great number of seal skins. The seal catcher was delighted, for such an order meant a large sum of money to him. But his face fell when the horseman added that it was absolutely necessary that the skins should be delivered that evening.

"I cannot do it," he said in a disappointed voice,

"for the seals will not come back to the rocks again until to-morrow morning."

"I can take you to a place where there are any number of seals," answered the stranger, "if you will mount behind me on my horse and come with me."

The seal catcher agreed to this, and climbed up behind the rider, who shook his bridle rein, and off the great horse galloped at such a pace that he had much ado to keep his seat.

On and on they went, flying like the wind, until at last they came to the edge of a huge precipice, the face of which went sheer down to the sea. Here the mysterious horseman pulled up his steed with a jerk.

"Get off now," he said shortly.

The seal catcher did as he was bid, and when he found himself safe on the ground, he peeped cautiously over the edge of the cliff, to see if there were any seals lying on the rocks below.

To his astonishment he saw no rocks, only the blue sea, which came right up to the foot of the cliff.

"Where are the seals that you spoke of?" he asked anxiously, wishing that he had never set out on such a rash adventure.

"You will see presently," answered the stranger, who was attending to his horse's bridle.

The seal catcher was now thoroughly frightened, for he felt sure that some evil was about to befall him, and in such a lonely place he knew that it would be useless to cry out for help.

And it seemed as if his fears would prove only too true, for the next moment the stranger's hand was laid upon his shoulder, and he felt himself being hurled bodily over the cliff, and then he fell with a splash into the sea.

He thought that his last hour had come, and he wondered how anyone could work such a deed of wrong upon an innocent man.

But, to his astonishment, he found that some change must have passed over him, for instead of being choked by the water, he could breathe quite easily, and he and his companion, who was still close at his side, seemed to be sinking as quickly down through the sea as they had flown through the air.

Down and down they went, nobody knows how far, till at last they came to a huge arched door, which appeared to be made of pink coral, studded over with cockle-shells. It opened, of its own accord, and when they entered they found themselves in a huge hall, the walls of which were formed of mother-of-pearl, and the floor of which was of sea-sand, smooth, and firm, and yellow.

The hall was crowded with occupants, but they were seals, not men, and when the seal catcher turned to his companion to ask him what it all meant, he was aghast to find that he, too, had assumed the form of a seal. He was still more aghast when he caught sight of himself in a large mirror that hung on the wall, and saw that he also no longer bore the likeness of a man, but was transformed into a nice, hairy, brown seal.

"Ah, woe to me," he said to himself, "for no fault of mine own this artful stranger hath laid some baneful charm upon me, and in this awful guise will I remain for the rest of my natural life."

At first none of the huge creatures spoke to him. For some reason or other they seemed to be very sad, and moved gently about the hall, talking quietly and mournfully to one another, or lay sadly upon the sandy floor, wiping big tears from their eyes with their soft furry fins.

But presently they began to notice him, and to whisper to one another, and presently his guide moved away from him, and disappeared through a door at the end of the hall. When he returned he held a huge knife in his hand.

"Didst thou ever see this before?" he asked, holding it out to the unfortunate seal catcher, who, to his horror, recognised his own hunting knife

with which he had struck the seal in the morning, and which had been carried off by the wounded animal.

At the sight of it he fell upon his face and begged for mercy, for he at once came to the conclusion that the inhabitants of the cavern, enraged at the harm which had been wrought upon their comrade, had, in some magic way, contrived to capture him, and to bring him down to their subterranean abode, in order to wreak their vengeance upon him by killing him.

But, instead of doing so, they crowded round him, rubbing their soft noses against his fur to show their sympathy, and implored him not to put himself about, for no harm would befall him, and they would love him all their lives long if he would only do what they asked him.

"Tell me what it is," said the seal catcher, "and I will do it, if it lies within my power."

"Follow me," answered his guide, and he led the way to the door through which he had disappeared when he went to seek the knife.

The seal catcher followed him. And there, in a smaller room, he found a great brown seal lying on a bed of pale pink sea-weed, with a gaping wound in his side.

"That is my father," said his guide, "whom thou

wounded this morning, thinking that he was one of the common seals who live in the sea, instead of a Merman who hath speech, and understanding, as you mortals have. I brought thee hither to bind up his wounds, for no other hand than thine can heal him."

"I have no skill in the art of healing," said the seal catcher, astonished at the forbearance of these strange creatures, whom he had so unwittingly wronged; "but I will bind up the wound to the best of my power, and I am only sorry that it was my hands that caused it."

He went over to the bed, and, stooping over the wounded Merman, washed and dressed the hurt as well as he could; and the touch of his hands appeared to work like magic, for no sooner had he finished than the wound seemed to deaden and die, leaving only the scar, and the old seal sprang up, as well as ever.

Then there was great rejoicing throughout the whole Palace of the Seals. They laughed, and they talked, and they embraced each other in their own strange way, crowding round their comrade, and rubbing their noses against his, as if to show him how delighted they were at his recovery.

But all this while the seal catcher stood alone in a corner, with his mind filled with dark thoughts,

for although he saw now that they had no intention of killing him, he did not relish the prospect of spending the rest of his life in the guise of a seal, fathoms deep under the ocean.

But presently, to his great joy, his guide approached him, and said, "Now you are at liberty to return home to your wife and children. I will take you to them, but only on one condition."

"And what is that?" asked the seal catcher eagerly, overjoyed at the prospect of being restored safely to the upper world, and to his family.

"That you will take a solemn oath never to wound a seal again."

"That will I do right gladly," he replied, for although the promise meant giving up his means of livelihood, he felt that if only he regained his proper shape he could always turn his hand to something else.

So he took the required oath with all due solemnity, holding up his fin as he swore, and all the other seals crowded round him as witnesses. And a sigh of relief went through the halls when the words were spoken, for he was the most noted seal catcher in the North.

Then he bade the strange company farewell, and, accompanied by his guide, passed once more through the outer doors of coral, and up, and up,

and up, through the shadowy green water, until it began to grow lighter and lighter and at last they emerged into the sunshine of earth.

Then, with one spring, they reached the top of the cliff, where the great black horse was waiting for them, quietly nibbling the green turf.

When they left the water their strange disguise dropped from them, and they were now as they had been before, a plain seal catcher and a tall, well-dressed gentleman in riding clothes.

"Get up behind me," said the latter, as he swung himself into his saddle. The seal catcher did as he was bid, taking tight hold of his companion's coat, for he remembered how nearly he had fallen off on his previous journey

Then it all happened as it happened before. The bridle was shaken, and the horse galloped off, and it was not long before the seal catcher found himself standing in safety before his own garden gate.

He held out his hand to say "good-bye," but as he did so the stranger pulled out a huge bag of gold and placed it in it.

"Thou hast done thy part of the bargain—we must do ours," he said. "Men shall never say that we took away an honest man's work without making reparation for it, and here is what will keep thee in comfort to thy life's end."

Then he vanished, and when the astonished seal catcher carried the bag into his cottage, and turned the gold out on the table, he found that what the stranger had said was true, and that he would be a rich man for the remainder of his days.

THE WANDERING OF ODYSSEUS

This next tale follows the adventures of the Ancient Greek hero Odysseus during his ten-year sea voyage home from the Trojan War – adapted here from Homer's Ancient Greek epic *The Odyssey* by nineteenth-century author Josephine Preston Peabody. While it is but one of the trials faced by Odysseus during his travels, the episode involving the sirens manages to nevertheless stand out. Although some modern incarnations have conflated the siren of antiquity with the fishtailed mermaid, likely due to the danger they both pose, the sirens of Ancient Greek mythology were distinct – appearing as human women with the legs and wings of a bird and using their voices to lure sailors to their death. While they crop up in Greek mythology quite regularly, Odysseus's method of escape has to be one of the most creative, a perfect example of why he is often remembered as Odysseus the Cunning.

Now Odysseus and his men sailed on and on till they came to Æolia, where dwells the king of the winds, and here they came nigh to good fortune.

Æolus received them kindly, and at their going he secretly gave to Odysseus a leathern bag in which all contrary winds were tied up securely, that only the favoring west wind might speed them to Ithaca. Nine days the ships went gladly before the wind, and on the tenth day they had sight of Ithaca, lying like a low cloud in the west. Then, so near his haven, the happy Odysseus gave up to his weariness and fell asleep, for he had never left the helm. But while he slept his men saw the leathern bag that he kept by him, and, in the belief that it was full of treasure, they opened it. Out rushed the ill-winds!

In an instant the sea was covered with white caps; the waves rose mountain high; the poor ships struggled against the tyranny of the gale and gave way. Back they were driven,—back, farther and farther; and when Odysseus woke, Ithaca was gone

from sight, as if it had indeed been only a low cloud in the west!

Straight to the island of Æolus they were driven once more. But when the king learned what greed and treachery had wasted his good gift, he would give them nothing more. "Surely thou must be a man hated of the gods, Odysseus," he said, "for misfortune bears thee company. Depart now; I may not help thee."

So, with a heavy heart, Odysseus and his men departed. For many days they rowed against a dead calm, until at length they came to the land of the Læstrygonians. And, to cut a piteous tale short, these giants destroyed all their fleet save one ship,— that of Odysseus himself, and in this he made escape to the island of Circe. What befell there, how the greedy seamen were turned into swine and turned back into men, and how the sorceress came to befriend Odysseus,—all this has been related.

There in Æaea the voyagers stayed a year before Circe would let them go. But at length she bade Odysseus seek the region of Hades, and ask of the sage Tiresias how he might ever return to Ithaca. How Odysseus followed this counsel, none may know; but by some mysterious journey, and with the aid of a spell, he came to the borders of Hades. There he saw and spoke with many

renowned Shades, old and young, even his own friends who had fallen on the plain of Troy. Achilles he saw, Patroclus and Ajax and Agamemnon, still grieving over the treachery of his wife. He saw, too, the phantom of Heracles, who lives with honor among the gods, and has for his wife Hebe, the daughter of Zeus and Juno. But though he would have talked with the heroes for a year and more, he sought out Tiresias.

"The anger of Poseidon follows thee," said the sage. "Wherefore, Odysseus, thy return is yet far off. But take heed when thou art come to Thrinacia, where the sacred kine of the Sun have their pastures. Do them no hurt, and thou shalt yet come home. *But if they be harmed in any wise*, ruin shall come upon thy men; and even if thou escape, thou shalt come home to find strange men devouring thy substance and wooing thy wife."

With this word in his mind, Odysseus departed and came once more to Æaea. There he tarried but a little time, till Circe had told him all the dangers that beset his way. Many a good counsel and crafty warning did she give him against the Sirens that charm with their singing, and against the monster Scylla and the whirlpool Charybdis, and the Clashing Rocks, and the cattle of the Sun. So the king and his men set out from the island of Æaea.

Now very soon they came to the Sirens who sing so sweetly that they lure to death every man who listens. For straightway he is mad to be with them where they sing; and alas for the man that would fly without wings!

But when the ship drew near the Sirens' island, Odysseus did as Circe had taught him. He bade all his shipmates stop up their ears with moulded wax, so that they could not hear. He alone kept his hearing; but he had himself lashed to the mast so that he could in no wise move, and he forbade them to loose him, however he might plead, under the spell of the Sirens.

As they sailed near, his soul gave way. He heard a wild sweetness coaxing the air, as a minstrel coaxes the harp; and there, close by, were the Sirens sitting in a blooming meadow that hid the bones of men. Beautiful, winning maidens they looked; and they sang, entreating Odysseus by name to listen and abide and rest. Their voices were golden-sweet above the sound of wind and wave, like drops of amber floating on the tide; and for all his wisdom, Odysseus strained at his bonds and begged his men to let him go free. But they, deaf alike to the song and the sorcery, rowed harder than ever. At length, song and island faded in the distance.

Odysseus came to his wits once more, and his men loosed his bonds and set him free.

But they were close upon new dangers. No sooner had they avoided the Clashing Rocks (by a device of Circe's) than they came to a perilous strait. On one hand they saw the whirlpool where, beneath a hollow fig-tree, Charybdis sucks down the sea horribly. And, while they sought to escape her, on the other hand monstrous Scylla upreared from the cave, snatched six of their company with her six long necks, and devoured them even while they called upon Odysseus to save them.

So, with bitter peril, the ship passed by and came to the island of Thrinacia; and here are goodly pastures for the flocks and herds of the Sun. Odysseus, who feared lest his men might forget the warning of Tiresias, was very loath to land. But the sailors were weary and worn to the verge of mutiny, and they swore, moreover, that they would never lay hands on the sacred kine. So they landed, thinking to depart next day. But with the next day came a tempest that blew for a month without ceasing, so that they were forced to beach the ship and live on the island with their store of corn and wine. When that was gone they had to hunt and fish, and it happened that, while Odysseus was absent in the woods one day, his shipmates broke

their oath. "For," said they, "when we are once more in Ithaca we will make amends to Helios with sacrifice. But let us rather drown than waste to death with hunger." So they drove off the best of the cattle of the Sun and slew them. When the king returned, he found them at their fateful banquet; but it was too late to save them from the wrath of the gods.

As soon as they were fairly embarked once more, the Sun ceased to shine. The sea rose high, the thunderbolt of Zeus struck that ship, and all its company was scattered abroad upon the waters. Not one was left save Odysseus. He clung to a fragment of his last ship, and so he drifted, borne here and there, and lashed by wind and wave, until he was washed up on the strand of the island Ogygia, the home of the nymph Calypso. He was not to leave this haven for seven years.

Here, after ten years of war and two of wandering, he found a kindly welcome. The enchanted island was full of wonders, and the nymph Calypso was more than mortal fair, and would have been glad to marry the hero; yet he pined for Ithaca. Nothing could win his heart away from his own country and his own wife Penelope, nothing but Lethe itself, and that no man may drink till he dies.

So for seven years Calypso strove to make him

forget his longing with ease and pleasant living and soft raiment. Day by day she sang to him while she broidered her web with gold; and her voice was like a golden strand that twines in and out of silence, making it beautiful. She even promised that she would make him immortal, if he would stay and be content; but he was heartsick for home.

At last his sorrow touched even the heart of Athena in heaven, for she loved his wisdom and his many devices. So she besought Zeus and all the other gods until they consented to shield Odysseus from the anger of Poseidon. Hermes himself bound on his winged sandals and flew down to Ogygia, where he found Calypso at her spinning. After many words, the nymph consented to give up her captive, for she was kind of heart, and all her graces had not availed to make him forget his home. With her help, Odysseus built a raft and set out upon his lonely voyage,—the only man remaining out of twelve good ships that had left Troy nigh unto ten years before.

The sea roughened against him, but (to shorten a tale of great peril) after many days, sore spent and tempest-tossed, he came to the land of the Phæacians, a land dear to the immortal gods, abounding in gifts of harvest and vintage, in god-like men and lovely women.

Here the shipwrecked king met the princess Nausicaa by the seaside, as she played ball with her maidens; and she, when she had heard of his plight, gave him food and raiment, and bade him follow her home. So he followed her to the palace of King Alcinous and Queen Arete, and abode with them, kindly refreshed, and honored with feasting and games and song. But it came to pass, as the minstrel sang before them of the Trojan War and the Wooden Horse, that Odysseus wept over the story, it was written so deep in his own heart. Then for the first time he told them his true name and all his trials.

They would gladly have kept so great a man with them forever, but they had no heart to keep him longer from his home; so they bade him farewell and set him upon one of their magical ships, with many gifts of gold and silver, and sent him on his way.

Wonderful seamen are the Phæacians. The ocean is to them as air to the bird,—the best path for a swift journey! Odysseus was glad enough to trust the way to them, and no sooner had they set out than a sweet sleep fell upon his eyelids. But the good ship sped like any bee that knows the way home. In a marvellous short time they came even to the shore of the kingdom of Ithaca.

While Odysseus was still sleeping, unconscious of his good fortune, the Phæacians lifted him from the ship with kindly joy and laid him upon his own shore; and beside him they set the gifts of gold and silver and fair work of the loom. So they departed; and thus it was that Odysseus came to Ithaca after twenty years.

PANIA OF THE REEF

This is the story of Pania as told by Tuiri Tareha, translated in *Te Ao Hou/The New World*, a bilingual Māori/English journal published by the Māori Affairs Department between 1952 and 1975. Pania herself is a figure of Māori folklore who hails from what is now the city of Napier in New Zealand – where you can visit her statue on the Marine Parade. She is also an example of how not all creatures of the sea have a fishy look about them. A mysterious woman of the sea, Pania passed her days beneath the waves, and her nights sat upon the shore observing the man that held her fascination. It is her son who ends up with fins and a tail in fact when he becomes a Taniwha – a spirit guardian of the waters who in his case takes on the shape of a shark.

Napier Breakwater (Kei tua te roanga atu) Pania

today is a ledge or reef of rock, commonly known now as the Napier breakwater, lying about four miles beyond Hukarere point. This was the home of Pania, a beautiful sea maiden who, in ancient times, daily swam shorewards at the setting of the sun and returned to her sea people before the break of day. While on shore she hid herself in a clump of flax beside a freshwater spring at the foot of Hukarere cliff, close by the sea. One evening a chief who lived in a nearby Pa became thirsty, and went for a drink at the spring. While drinking from his calabash he spied Pania sitting in the middle of the flax bush. There and then he took her to his home, and they became man and wife. But always, every morning, Pania would return to her sea folk and every evening come back to her husband. After awhile Pania gave birth to a son who was completely without hair and so was named Maremare, 'the hairless one.' With the birth of this child, Pania's husband became concerned that he might

lose him to the sea people. So he consulted a tohunga, in the hope of finding how to keep his child and wife with him always. The tohunga told him to place cooked food upon the mother and child while they slept, and they would never again return to the sea. Evidently something went amiss. Perhaps the food was not properly cooked; for Pania returned to her people never to return. The child Moremore was turned to a shark (taniwha) which lived in the waters around the reef off Hukarere, and at Rangatira, the entrance to the inner harbour at the delta of the river called Ahuriri. When fishermen of today tell the legend of Pania, they claim that at ebb-tide she may be seen lying outstretched at the bottom of the rocky shelf, with her hair still as black as ever and her arms stretched shoreward. According to old Maori folk, however, she was turned into a fishing rock, from which various kinds of fish might be caught. Within the hollow of her left arm-pit only rawaru may be caught, and from her right arm-pit snapper alone, while her thighs yield only the hapuka. In the days of old these fishing grounds were sacred, but today, being frequented by pakehas, the place has become common to all and fish are no longer plentiful.

THE ENCHANTED FISH

'The Enchanted Fish' – alternatively titled 'The Girl Fish' – is a Catalan folk-tale originally found in Francisco Maspons y Labrós's nineteenth-century collection *Cuentos Populars Catalans*. This translated version, however, is another that was recorded by twentieth-century folklorist Andrew Lang in *The Orange Fairy Book*. The story itself is one that contains, you guessed it, an enchanted fish – a not altogether uncommon trope in fairy tales from around the world (for example, the Grimm's tale 'The Fisherman and his Wife'). It is the perfect reminder that while many of the legendary creatures featured in this book take humanoid shapes, even if not in their entirety, those animals beneath the water that might instead appear perfectly normal can be equally as magical – so, best not to get on their bad side.

Once upon a time there lived on the bank of a stream a man and a woman and their daughter. As she was an only child, and very pretty besides, they never could make up their minds to punish her for her faults or to teach her nice manners; and as for work—she laughed in her mother's face if she asked her to help cook the dinner or to wash the plates. All the girl would do was to spend her days in dancing and playing with her friends; and for any use she was to her parents they might as well have had no daughter at all.

However, one morning her mother looked so tired that even the selfish girl could not help seeing it and asked if there was anything she was able to do, so that her mother might rest a little.

The good woman looked so surprised and grateful for this offer that the girl felt rather ashamed, and at that moment would have scrubbed down the house if she had been requested. But her mother only begged her to take the fishing net out

to the bank of the river and mend some holes in it as her father intended to go fishing that night.

The girl took the net and worked so hard that soon there was not a hole to be found. She felt quite pleased with herself, though she had had plenty to amuse her, as everybody who passed by had stopped and had a chat with her. But by this time the sun was high over head, and she was just folding her net to carry it home again, when she heard a splash behind her, and looking round she saw a big fish jump into the air. Seizing the net with both hands, she flung it into the water where the circles were spreading one behind the other, and more by luck than skill drew out the fish.

'Well, you are a beauty!' she cried to herself.

But the fish looked up to her and said, 'You had better not kill me, for if you do, I will turn you into a fish yourself!'

The girl laughed contemptuously and ran straight in to her mother.

'Look what I have caught,' she said gaily. 'But it is almost a pity to eat it, for it can talk, and it declares that if I kill it, it will turn me into a fish too.'

'Oh put it back, put it back!' implored the mother. 'Perhaps it is skilled in magic. And I should die, and so would your father, if anything should happen to you.'

'Oh, nonsense, mother; what power could a creature like that have over me? Besides, I am hungry, and if I don't have my dinner very soon, I shall be cross.' And off she went to gather some flowers to stick in her hair.

About an hour later the blowing of a horn told her that dinner was ready.

'Didn't I say that fish would be delicious?' she cried, and plunging her spoon into the dish the girl helped herself to a large piece. But the instant it touched her mouth a cold shiver ran through her. Her head seemed to flatten, and her eyes to look oddly round the corners; her legs and her arms were stuck to her sides, and she gasped wildly for breath. With a mighty bound she sprang through the window and fell into the river, where she soon felt better and was able to swim to the sea, which was close by.

No sooner had she arrived there than the sight of her sad face attracted the notice of some of the other fishes, and they pressed round her, begging her to tell them her story.

'I am not a fish at all,' said the newcomer, swallowing a great deal of salt water as she spoke, for you cannot learn how to be a proper fish all in a moment. 'I am not a fish at all, but a girl; at least I was a girl a few minutes ago, only—' And she

ducked her head under the waves so that they should not see her crying.

'Only you did not believe that the fish you caught had power to carry out its threat,' said an old tunny. 'Well, never mind, that has happened to all of us, and it really is not a bad life. Cheer up and come with us and see our queen, who lives in a palace that is much more beautiful than any your queens can boast of.'

The new fish felt a little afraid of taking such a journey, but as she was still more afraid of being left alone, she waved her tail in token of consent, and off they all set, hundreds of them together.

The people on the rocks and in the ships that saw them pass said to each other, 'Look what a splendid shoal!' They had no idea that they were hastening to the queen's palace, but, then, dwellers on land have so little notion of what goes on in the bottom of the sea! Certainly the little new fish had none. She had watched jelly-fish and nautilus swimming a little way below the surface, and beautiful coloured seaweeds floating about; but that was all. Now, when she plunged deeper her eyes fell upon strange things.

Wedges of gold, great anchors, heaps of pearl, inestimable stones, unvalued jewels—all scattered in the bottom of the sea! Dead men's bones were

there also, and long white creatures who had never seen the light, for they mostly dwelt in the clefts of rocks where the sun's rays could not come. At first our little fish felt as if she were blind also, but by-and-by she began to make out one object after another in the green dimness, and by the time she had swum for a few hours all became clear.

'Here we are at last,' cried a big fish, going down into a deep valley, for the sea has its mountains and valleys just as much as the land. 'That is the palace of the queen of the fishes, and I think you must confess that the emperor himself has nothing so fine.'

'It is beautiful indeed,' gasped the little fish, who was very tired with trying to swim as fast as the rest, and beautiful beyond words the palace was. The walls were made of pale pink coral, worn smooth by the waters, and round the windows were rows of pearls; the great doors were standing open, and the whole troop floated into a chamber of audience, where the queen, who was half a woman after all, was seated on a throne made of a green and blue shell.

'Who are you, and where do you come from?' she asked the little fish, whom the others had pushed in front. And in a low, trembling voice, the visitor told her story.

'I was once a girl too,' answered the queen, when the fish had ended, 'and my father was the king of a great country. A husband was found for me, and on my wedding day my mother placed her crown on my head and told me that as long as I wore it I should likewise be queen. For many months I was as happy as a girl could be, especially when I had a little son to play with. But, one morning, when I was walking in my gardens, there came a giant and snatched the crown from my head. Holding me fast, he told me that he intended to give the crown to his daughter, and to enchant my husband the prince, so that he should not know the difference between us. Since then she has filled my place and been queen in my stead. As for me, I was so miserable that I threw myself into the sea, and my ladies, who loved me, declared that they would die too. But, instead of dying, some wizard, who pitied my fate, turned us all into fishes, though he allowed me to keep the face and body of a woman. And fishes we must remain till someone brings me back my crown again!'

'I will bring it back if you will tell me what to do!' cried the little fish; who would have promised anything that was likely to carry her up to earth again.

The queen answered: 'Yes, I will tell you what to do.' She sat silent for a moment, and then went on:

'There is no danger if you will only follow my counsel; first you must return to earth and go up to the top of a high mountain, where the giant has built his castle. You will find him sitting on the steps weeping for his daughter, who has just died while the prince was away hunting. At the last she sent her father my crown by a faithful servant. But I warn you to be careful, for if he sees you he may kill you. Therefore I will give you the power to change yourself into any creature that may help you best. You have only to strike your forehead and call out its name.'

This time the journey to land seemed much shorter than before, and when once the fish reached the shore she struck her forehead sharply with her tail, and cried:

'Deer, come to me.'

In a moment the small fish body disappeared, and in its place stood a beautiful beast with branching horns and slender legs, quivering with longing to be gone. Throwing back her head and snuffing the air, she broke into a run, leaping easily over the rivers and walls that stood in her way.

It happened that the king's son had been

hunting since daybreak, but had killed nothing, and when the deer crossed his path as he was resting under a tree he determined to have it. He flung himself on his horse, which went like the wind, and as the prince had often hunted the forest before, and knew all the short cuts, he at last came up with the panting beast.

'By your favour let me go, and do not kill me,' said the deer, turning to the prince with tears in her eyes, 'for I have far to run and much to do.' And as the prince, struck dumb with surprise, only looked at her, the deer cleared the next wall and was soon out of sight.

'That can't really be a deer,' said the prince to himself, reining in his horse and not attempting to follow her. 'No deer ever had eyes like that. It must be an enchanted maiden, and I will marry her and no other.'

So, turning his horse's head, he rode slowly back to his palace.

The deer reached the giant's castle quite out of breath, and her heart sank as she gazed at the tall, smooth walls which surrounded it. Then she plucked up courage and cried:

'Ant, come to me!' And in a moment the branching horns and beautiful shape had vanished,

and a tiny brown ant, invisible to all who did not look closely, was climbing up the walls.

It was wonderful how fast she went, that little creature! The wall must have appeared miles high in comparison with her own body; yet, in less time than would have seemed possible, she was over the top and down in the courtyard on the other side. Here she paused to consider what had best be done next, and looking about her she saw that one of the walls had a tall tree growing by it, and in this corner was a window very nearly on a level with the highest branches of the tree.

'Monkey, come to me!' cried the ant; and before you could turn round a monkey was swinging herself from the topmost branches into the room where the giant lay snoring.

Perhaps he will be so frightened at the sight of me that he may die of fear, and I shall never get the crown, thought the monkey. I had better become something else. And she called softly, 'Parrot, come to me!'

Then a pink and gray parrot hopped up to the giant, who by this time was stretching himself and giving yawns which shook the castle. The parrot waited a little until he was really awake, and then she said boldly that she had been sent to take away

the crown, which was not his any longer, now his daughter the queen was dead.

On hearing these words the giant leapt out of bed with an angry roar, and sprang at the parrot in order to wring her neck with his great hands. But the bird was too quick for him and, flying behind his back, begged the giant to have patience, as her death would be of no use to him.

'That is true,' answered the giant, 'but I am not so foolish as to give you that crown for nothing. Let me think what I will have in exchange!' And he scratched his huge head for several minutes, for giants' minds always move slowly.

'Ah, yes, that will do!' exclaimed the giant at last, his face brightening. 'You shall have the crown if you will bring me a collar of blue stones from the Arch of St. Martin, in the great City.'

Now when the parrot had been a girl she had often heard of this wonderful arch and the precious stones and marbles that had been let into it. It sounded as if it would be a very hard thing to get them away from the building of which they formed a part, but all had gone well with her so far, and at any rate she could but try. So she bowed to the giant, and made her way back to the window where the giant could not see her. Then she called quickly:

'Eagle, come to me!'

Before she had even reached the tree she felt herself borne up on strong wings ready to carry her to the clouds if she wished to go there and, seeming a mere speck in the sky, she was swept along till she beheld the Arch of St. Martin far below, with the rays of the sun shining on it. Then she swooped down and, hiding herself behind a buttress so that she could not be detected from below, she set herself to dig out the nearest blue stones with her beak. It was even harder work than she had expected; but at last it was done, and hope arose in her heart. She next drew out a piece of string that she had found hanging from a tree, and sitting down to rest strung the stones together.

When the necklace was finished she hung it round her neck, and called, 'Parrot, come to me!' And a little later the pink and gray parrot stood before the giant.

'Here is the necklace you asked for,' said the parrot. The eyes of the giant glistened as he took the heap of blue stones in his hand. But for all that he was not minded to give up the crown.

'They are hardly as blue as I expected,' he grumbled, though the parrot knew as well as he did that he was not speaking the truth. 'You must bring me something else in exchange for the crown

you covet so much. If you fail it will cost you not only the crown but your life also.'

'What is it you want now?' asked the parrot; and the giant answered:

'If I give you my crown I must have another still more beautiful. This time you shall bring me a crown of stars.'

The parrot turned away, and as soon as she was outside she murmured, 'Toad, come to me!' And sure enough a toad she was, and off she set in search of the starry crown.

She had not gone far before she came to a clear pool, in which the stars were reflected so brightly that they looked quite real to touch and handle. Stooping down she filled a bag she was carrying with the shining water and, returning to the castle wove a crown out of the reflected stars. Then she cried as before:

'Parrot, come to me!' And in the shape of a parrot she entered the presence of the giant.

'Here is the crown you asked for,' she said.

And this time the giant could not help crying out with admiration. He knew he was beaten, and still holding the chaplet of stars, he turned to the girl.

'Your power is greater than mine: take the crown; you have won it fairly!'

The parrot did not need to be told twice. Seizing the crown, she sprang on to the window, crying, 'Monkey, come to me!" And for a monkey, the climb down the tree into the courtyard did not take half a minute.

When she had reached the ground she said again, 'Ant, come to me!' And a little ant at once began to crawl over the high wall. How glad the ant was to be out of the giant's castle, holding fast the crown which had shrunk into almost nothing, as she herself had done, but grew quite big again when the ant exclaimed, 'Deer, come to me!'

Surely no deer ever ran so swiftly as that one! On and on she went, bounding over rivers and crashing through tangles till she reached the sea. Here she cried, for the last time:

'Fish come to me!' And, plunging in, she swam along the bottom as far as the palace, where the queen and all the fishes were gathered together awaiting her.

The hours since she had left had gone very slowly—as they always do to people who are waiting—and many of them had quite given up hope.

'I am tired of staying here,' grumbled a beautiful little creature, whose colours changed with every movement of her body, 'I want to see what is

going on in the upper world. It must be months since that fish went away.'

'It was a very difficult task, and the giant must certainly have killed her or she would have been back long ago,' remarked another.

'The young flies will be coming out now,' murmured a third, 'and they will all be eaten up by the river fish! It is really too bad!'

Suddenly, a voice was heard from behind, 'Look! Look! What is that bright thing moving so swiftly toward us?' And the queen started up, and stood on her tail, so excited was she.

A silence fell on all the crowd, and even the grumblers held their peace and gazed with the rest. On and on came the fish, holding the crown tightly in her mouth, and the others moved back to let her pass. On she went right up to the queen, who bent down, and taking the crown, placed it on her own head.

Then a wonderful thing happened. Her tail dropped away or, rather, it divided and grew into two legs and a pair of the prettiest feet in the world, while her maidens, who were grouped around her, shed their scales and became girls again. They all turned and looked at each other first, and next at the little fish who had regained her own shape and was more beautiful than any of them.

'It is you who have given us back our life! You, you!' they cried, and fell to weeping for very joy.

So they all went back to earth and the queen's palace, and quite forgot the one that lay under the sea. But they had been so long away that they found many changes. The prince, the queen's husband, had died some years since, and in his place was her son, who had grown up and was king! Even in his joy at seeing his mother again an air of sadness clung to him, and at last the queen could bear it no longer, and begged him to walk with her in the garden. Seated together in a bower of jessamine—where she had passed long hours as a bride—she took her son's hand and entreated him to tell her the cause of his sorrow. 'For,' said she, 'if I can give you happiness you shall have it.'

'It is no use,' answered the prince, 'nobody can help me. I must bear it alone.'

'But at least let me share your grief,' urged the queen.

'No one can do that,' said he. 'I have fallen in love with one I can never marry, and I must get on as best I can.'

'It may not be so impossible as you think,' answered the queen. 'At any rate, tell me.'

There was silence between them for a moment,

then, turning away his head, the prince answered gently:

'I have fallen in love with a beautiful deer!'

'Ah, if that is all,' exclaimed the queen joyfully. And she told him that, as he had guessed, it was no deer but an enchanted maiden who had won back the crown and brought her home to her own people.

'She is here, in my palace,' added the queen. 'I will take you to her.'

But when the prince stood before the girl, who was so much more beautiful than anything he had ever dreamed of, he lost all his courage, and stood with bent head before her.

Then the maiden drew near, and her eyes as she looked at him were the eyes of the deer that day in the forest. She whispered softly:

'By your favour let me go, and do not kill me.'

The prince remembered her words, and his heart was filled with happiness. And the queen, his mother, watched them and smiled.

THE TUNA (EEL) OF LAKE VAIHIRIA

The next story tells the tale of the Polynesian princess Hina, daughter of the sun and moon. This tale, specifically, is what is often known as an origin myth – a story that explains how and why parts of our world are the way they are – in this case for the coconut tree. There are actually numerous variations on the story of Hina across Polynesia, varying from culture to culture, but which all share the same common thread: the origin of this important plant. The version you are about to read here originates from Tahiti and was written down by Teuria Henry and published by the museum of Honolulu in 1928. Henry in turn based a lot of her research on the records of J. M. Osmond, who credits the story of Hina as he received it to a Madame Butteaud, a descendant of the Hina of said legend. Truly, this is a tale that insists on being shared.

There was once a beautiful young princess of Papeuriri, Tahiti, of the highest lineage, whose celestial patrons, the sun and moon, had named her Hina (Gray). When this young girl had reached the stature of womanhood and was becoming much admired for her beauty—flashes of light emanating from her person restricted her to a very select circle—the sun and moon espoused her to the king of Lake Vaihiria, before she had any personal acquaintance with him or her even seen him. The king's name was Fa'arava'ai-anu (Cause-to-fish-in-the-cold), and as her parents agreed to the marriage Hina felt no doubt of the suitableness of the match and entered happily into all the preparations for her wedding. Hina chose for her maids of honor, two childhood companions, named Varua (Spirit) and Te-roro (Brain), and when at last the marriage day arrived they were attractively dressed in white tapa gracefully wound around their persons, with garlands of maire fern interwoven with red *fara* strobile tips and snow-white *tiare*,

and in their flowing raven hair they entwined similar wreaths. The bride also wore, in token of her rank, a necklet and girdle of rich red and yellow *'ura* (parrakeet feathers).

At length the bridal party set out to meet the bridegroom, accompanied with the measured beat of the drum and the soft notes of the bamboo flute and other musical instruments, and they had gone half way up the valley to Lake Vaihiria, when, lo, the bridegroom was seen descending the declivity to meet them. And there in the distance Hina saw to her great horror, an immense eel, as great and long as the trunk of a tall coconut tree; this was Fa'arava'aianu, king of Lake Vaihiria, the intended bridegroom for the beautiful Hina!

Terror-stricken, she turned to her parents and exclaimed: "It is indeed this, O my parents? Do you wish me to be wedded to a monster and not a person? O how cruel of you! And now I shall seek my own salvation!" And she fled out of the valley to her home.

On arriving there, the people were surprised to see her and enquired what had happened. On knowing her grief and disappointment, sorrow and sympathy filled their hearts towards her.

"And now," she said, "farewell. I must seek my salvation quickly away from here. If all be well, I

shall return again; but meanwhile, my dear friends, I entrust all my treasures to your care. If I live, I shall return to my own district, to be with you, my dearly loved ones."

Willing hands quickly prepared a swift canoe, and just as the moon was rising in its full glory, Hina, with trusted retainers, set off for Vairao, Taiarapu, to seek the aid and protection of the great Mâ-û-i who had noosed and controlled the sun, and there they arrived just before daybreak.

On entering his cave, Hina found Mâ-û-i was out, but she was kindly received by his wife. Shortly afterwards he came in and enquired of his wife what caused the brilliant flashes of light in their dark abode, and she replied:

"This is Hina of the *'ura* girdle, Hina of lightning flashes in' the east, Hina, child of the sun and moon; her wind is the northeast trade wind."

Then Mâ-û-i welcomed Hina, and kindly addressed her saying, "O Hina, beloved daughter of Mataica, what is your errand, my Princess?"

"O Mâ-û-i," she exclaimed, "save me from the hideous monster, the king of Vaihiria, who will be coming here to claim me as his wife! Have pity on me, behold now outside, and what is the wind? It is possessed, darkness is overshadowing the land, and the sea is foaming so that the ocean beyond

cannot be seen?" And then, while Hina told her sad story, they saw the eel king breaking an entrance passage in the reef.

Mâ-û-i was horrified, and he hastened to place his two stone gods upon the cliffs and to sharpen his axe and make ready his fishhook for action. Then, as the eel was approaching the shore, Mâ-û-i placed some tempting bait upon the fishhook and secured it with Hina's hair.

As soon as the eel saw him, he roared out in a thundering voice, "Mâ-û-i, deliver me my bride!"

And Mâ-û-i cast his fishhook into the sea, saying, "This is I, Mâ-û-i the brave! No king can escape me here in my heritage; he will become food for my images."

Then the eel perceiving the food, opened wide his mouth and swallowed the fishhook and bait, and soon Mâ-û-i drew him up on to the shore. He chopped off his great head, which he wrapped in tapa, and presented it to Hina, saying:

"Hold this, and put it not down an instant until you arrive home; then take and plant it in the center of your marae ground. This eel's head contains for you great treasures; from it you will have material to build and complete your house, besides food to eat and water to drink. But remember my warning, that you lose not your valuable property by putting

it down before you reach home. Then you will ever be remembered as Hina-vahine-e-anapa-te-uira-i-te-Hiti'a-o-te-ra (Hina-of-lightning-flashes-in-the-east)."

So Hina took the great bundle, which became light by magic, and sending on her canoe along the coast, she and an attendant maid preferred walking a few miles. So they went on their way rejoicing, and arrived at a place called Pani (To-close), where they saw a nice deep stream of water, at which they stopped to drink. In doing this, Hina thoughtlessly put down her bundle. Soon the two girls made up their minds to take a bath. So in they plunged and dove first upwards in the stream and then downwards, when Hina all at once remembered her eel's head and left the water quickly to go and take it up again. But lo, as she approached it, she found the tapa removed, and there the head stood erect, rooted to the ground and sprouting! It had become a young coconut tree. Then Hina saw and understood why Mâ-û-i had told her only to put it down at her own marae, and she wept bitterly.

Just then a woman of the people, but of good standing in the land, came along and enquired of the girl her trouble, and when Hina told her, the woman whose name was Rû-roa (Great-haste), said comfortingly:

"Be not troubled for this land is ours; come and sojourn with me so as to watch the growth of your new tree, which shall always be yours."

Hina, comforted, accepted the woman's kind invitation, and after sending her companion on to the canoe with word for her people to return home, she committed herself to the care of her new friend, who soon made her very comfortable in her home not far off.

After partaking of a hearty breakfast, Hina threw herself down upon a mat, and fell asleep, which rest she needed, and towards evening as she awoke, she heard voices outside not far from the house. Looking out she perceived two handsome young men, sons of Rû-roa, who had been out fishing; and she heard them enquire of their mother as to the cause of flashes of lightning that they saw coming out of their dwelling, to which she replied:

"It is Hina, princess of Papeuriri, and child of the sun and moon. She has a young coconut tree growing yonder, which she is staying here to watch until it matures."

Awe-struck, the young men would not enter the house but remained outside. The younger brother went to see the new tree, and found it loaded with coconuts. So he picked one and husked it and took

it to his mother and brother, and while they were examining and admiring it, Hina, wishing to place them all at ease in her presence, called to them to come in. She said to the elder brother:

"Your name must be Mahana-e-anapa-i-te-po'ipo'i" (Sun-that-flashes-in-the-morning). And to the younger brother she said: "You must be called Ava'e-e-hiti-i-te-ahiahi" (Moon-that-rises-in-the-evening).

By giving them these names, which plebeians never dared to adopt in times of yore, she created them nobles, an act which also gave rank to their mother. Thus united in bonds of friendship, they all lived happily together, the family being charmed with the beautiful and affable Hina, and they enjoyed eating the coconuts, which had become the admiration of all Tai'arapu.

Hina and Mahana-e-anapa-i-te-po'ipo'i became much attached to each other, and they were married, and in due time she had a daughter whom they named Te-ipo-o-te-marama (Pet-of-the-moon). But to her great sorrow Hina's husband soon died. She afterwards married the younger brother, who reminded her much of her deceased husband, and by him she had another daughter, whom they named Te-ipo-o-te-here (Pet-who-loved).

One day, as each child held a matured coconut in her hand, they were caught up by the gods on to a rainbow, by which they were conducted to Takahoro, in the atoll of Ana (Chain Island), in the Tuamotus. The younger sister, finding that her coconut was without water, changed it for that of her elder sister, unbeknown to her, which displeased the gods; and causing her to drop the coconut, which was sprouting, they carried her away in the clouds, and she was never seen again. So Te-ipo-o-te-marama became the sole owner of this, the first coconut tree that grew at Ana, from which were produced all the coconut trees that have spread throughout the group and have developed into many varieties. The tree stood, towering high above all other trees of the group, until the cyclone of February 8, 1906, broke it off in three pieces, which were washed away by the sea.

Hina lived long and happily with her husband, sometimes in Tai'arapu, sometimes in Pape'uriri, and she had numerous issue.

GLAUCUS AND SCYLLA

Move aside Poseidon, move aside Triton, there is a new god of the sea in town: Glaucus. According to Greek mythology, Glaucus was a minor sea god who began life as a mortal fisherman. His transformation to watery deity could not have been more complete, however, bestowing him with a familiar merman-like fishtail in place of his legs. Here Glaucus's story is narrated by twentieth-century writer Emilie Kip Baker and is presumably (based on their similarities) adapted from the most complete narration of this tale that survives from antiquity: Ovid's *Metamorphoses*, a first-century Roman poem. Although, it is perhaps unfair to simply call this the story of Glaucus, for it is also the story of Scylla – a mortal woman whose encounter with divinity is far less triumphant than Glaucus's own rise to power.

One of the many sea-gods who ruled under Neptune was Glaucus, who was once a poor fisherman, and earned his living by selling the fish that he caught each day. One morning he had an extra large haul; and when he threw the fish on the ground beside him, he noticed that they were eagerly nibbling the grass that grew very thickly in the spot where he had flung his net. As he stood watching them, the fish suddenly leaped up from the ground; and having flopped back into the water, swam away. Curious to see whether it was the grass that gave them this extraordinary power, Glauous chewed a bit of it himself, and immediately he felt an irresistible desire to plunge into the sea. Fearlessly he dived beneath the waves, and soon found no difficulty in keeping under water, for the ocean seemed now to be his native element. He saw his beard turning a lovely sea-green; and he found that his hair, grown suddenly long and green, was trailing out behind him. His arms were azure-colored, and his legs became a fish's tail; but

he felt no regrets over losing his human form, and stayed contentedly in the ocean. In time Neptune made him one of the lesser gods, and took him into the friendly fraternity of the sea.

As Glaucus was swimming one day near the shore, he saw a beautiful maiden named Scylla; and fell so much in love with her that he forgot he was half fish, and begged her to be his wife. Scylla stared at his green hair and blue skin, but this did not frighten her, nor did she wonder at his fish's tail; for she had often played with the sea-nymphs, and was accustomed to their strange appearance. Glaucus felt encouraged by her behavior, and begged her to listen to the story of his life. He told her how he had suffered a sea change, and now occupied the lofty position of a god. The maiden was interested in this recital, but she had no desire to marry a merman, even if he were a god; so when Glaucus ventured to come nearer to her, she turned and fled. Discouraged but still determined, the young god sought the aid of the enchantress Circe, and begged her to give him some love-potion by which he might win the unwilling Scylla. Circe was so well pleased with the handsome sea-god that she urged him to accept her love, and forget the maiden who scorned him; but Glaucus would not yield to the persuasions of

the enchantress, and kept pleading for the desired love-potion.

Seeing that she could not gain his affections, Circe determined that at least no one else should enjoy his love; so she refused to make the potion, and sent Glaucus angrily away. When she saw him go sorrowfully from her palace, she mixed a magic liquid, brewed from poisonous plants and deadly weeds, and this she poured over the waters where Scylla was wont to bathe. The maiden, suspecting no treachery, sought the ocean at her accustomed hour, and as soon as the poisoned waves touched her body she became a horrible monster with six heads—each having three rows of sharp teeth. She saw all around her serpents and barking dogs that were part of her own body, which had suddenly become rooted to the spot where she stood. She never regained her human form, but stayed in this place forever to terrify all mariners, and to devour the hapless sailors that came within her reach. Opposite her was the den of Charybdis, who three times a day swallowed the waters of the sea, and three times threw them up again. On the rock above the den was an immense fir-tree, and all ships that passed that way watched eagerly for this signal of danger, and prayed that they might safely

steer between the double horrors of Scylla and Charybdis.

> "There Scylla dwells,
> And fills the air with fearful yells; her voice
> The cry of whelps just littered, but herself
> A frightful prodigy—a sight which none
> Would care to look on, though he were a god.
> Twelve feet are hers, all shapeless; six long necks,
> A hideous head on each, and triple rows
> Of teeth, close set and many, threatening death.
> And forth from that dark gulf her heads are thrust,
> To look abroad upon the rocks for prey,—
> ... No mariner can boast
> That he has passed by Scylla with a crew
> Unharmed."
>
> —Bryant's Homer's *Odyssey*, Book XII, line 100.

THE LITTLE MERMAID

Perhaps you've gotten this far and wondered how I could compile a collection of merfolk tales and *not* include 'The Little Mermaid'? I couldn't, that's how. First penned by Danish writer Hans Christian Andersen, the tale of 'The Little Mermaid' has been adapted for page, screen, and stage countless times since 1837, and many of you will have likely encountered at least one variation on the original in your lifetime. Still, Andersen's story is always worth reading for yourself thanks to its complex layers, emotive themes, and literary influence. Potentially far more tragic than you've come to expect, the story of 'The Little Mermaid' is believed by scholars to be an exploration of unrequited love inspired by Andersen's own feelings towards his friend Jonas Collins, a Danish civil servant; in response to Collins's wedding, Andersen penned this tale of longing and loneliness that has continued to speak to readers throughout the centuries since.

Far out in the ocean the water is as blue as the petals of the loveliest cornflower, and as clear as the purest glass. But it is very deep too. It goes down deeper than any anchor rope will go, and many, many steeples would have to be stacked one on top of another to reach from the bottom to the surface of the sea. It is down there that the sea folk live.

Now don't suppose that there are only bare white sands at the bottom of the sea. No indeed! The most marvelous trees and flowers grow down there, with such pliant stalks and leaves that the least stir in the water makes them move about as though they were alive. All sorts of fish, large and small, dart among the branches, just as birds flit through the trees up here. From the deepest spot in the ocean rises the palace of the sea king. Its walls are made of coral and its high pointed windows of the clearest amber, but the roof is made of mussel shells that open and shut with the tide. This is a wonderful sight to see, for every shell holds

glistening pearls, any one of which would be the pride of a queen's crown.

The sea king down there had been a widower for years, and his old mother kept house for him. She was a clever woman, but very proud of her noble birth. Therefore she flaunted twelve oysters on her tail while the other ladies of the court were only allowed to wear six. Except for this she was an altogether praiseworthy person, particularly so because she was extremely fond of her granddaughters, the little sea princesses. They were six lovely girls, but the youngest was the most beautiful of them all. Her skin was as soft and tender as a rose petal, and her eyes were as blue as the deep sea, but like all the others she had no feet. Her body ended in a fish tail.

The whole day long they used to play in the palace, down in the great halls where live flowers grew on the walls. Whenever the high amber windows were thrown open the fish would swim in, just as swallows dart into our rooms when we open the windows. But these fish, now, would swim right up to the little princesses to eat out of their hands and let themselves be petted.

Outside the palace was a big garden, with flaming red and deep-blue trees. Their fruit glittered like gold, and their blossoms flamed like fire on

their constantly waving stalks. The soil was very fine sand indeed, but as blue as burning brimstone. A strange blue veil lay over everything down there. You would have thought yourself aloft in the air with only the blue sky above and beneath you, rather than down at the bottom of the sea. When there was a dead calm, you could just see the sun, like a scarlet flower with light streaming from its calyx.

Each little princess had her own small garden plot, where she could dig and plant whatever she liked. One of them made her little flower bed in the shape of a whale, another thought it neater to shape hers like a little mermaid, but the youngest of them made hers as round as the sun, and there she grew only flowers which were as red as the sun itself. She was an unusual child, quiet and wistful, and when her sisters decorated their gardens with all kinds of odd things they had found in sunken ships, she would allow nothing in hers except flowers as red as the sun, and a pretty marble statue. This figure of a handsome boy, carved in pure white marble, had sunk down to the bottom of the sea from some ship that was wrecked. Beside the statue she planted a rose-colored weeping willow tree, which thrived so well that its graceful branches shaded the statue and hung down to the

blue sand, where their shadows took on a violet tint, and swayed as the branches swayed. It looked as if the roots and the tips of the branches were kissing each other in play.

Nothing gave the youngest princess such pleasure as to hear about the world of human beings up above them. Her old grandmother had to tell her all she knew about ships and cities, and of people and animals. What seemed nicest of all to her was that up on land the flowers were fragrant, for those at the bottom of the sea had no scent. And she thought it was nice that the woods were green, and that the fish you saw among their branches could sing so loud and sweet that it was delightful to hear them. Her grandmother had to call the little birds "fish," or the princess would not have known what she was talking about, for she had never seen a bird.

"When you get to be fifteen," her grandmother said, "you will be allowed to rise up out of the ocean and sit on the rocks in the moonlight, to watch the great ships sailing by. You will see woods and towns, too."

Next year one of her sisters would be fifteen, but the others – well, since each was a whole year older than the next the youngest still had five long years to wait until she could rise up from the water

and see what our world was like. But each sister promised to tell the others about all that she saw, and what she found most marvelous on her first day. Their grandmother had not told them half enough, and there were so many things that they longed to know about. The most eager of them all was the youngest, the very one who was so quiet and wistful. Many a night she stood by her open window and looked up through the dark blue water where the fish waved their fins and tails. She could just see the moon and stars. To be sure, their light was quite dim, but looked at through the water they seemed much bigger than they appear to us. Whenever a cloud-like shadow swept across them, she knew that it was either a whale swimming overhead, or a ship with many human beings aboard it. Little did they dream that a pretty young mermaid was down below, stretching her white arms up toward the keel of their ship.

The eldest princess had her fifteenth birthday, so now she received permission to rise up out of the water. When she got back she had a hundred things to tell her sisters about, but the most marvelous thing of all, she said, was to lie on a sand bar in the moonlight, when the sea was calm, and to gaze at the large city on the shore, where the lights twinkled like hundreds of stars; to listen to

music; to hear the chatter and clamor of carriages and people; to see so many church towers and spires; and to hear the ringing bells. Because she could not enter the city, that was just what she most dearly longed to do.

Oh, how intently the youngest sister listened. After this, whenever she stood at her open window at night and looked up through the dark blue waters, she thought of that great city with all of its clatter and clamor, and even fancied that in these depths she could hear the church bells ring.

The next year, her second sister had permission to rise up to the surface and swim wherever she pleased. She came up just at sunset, and she said that this spectacle was the most marvelous sight she had ever seen. The heavens had a golden glow, and as for the clouds – she could not find words to describe their beauty. Splashed with red and tinted with violet, they sailed over her head. But much faster than the sailing clouds were wild swans in a flock. Like a long white veil trailing above the sea, they flew toward the setting sun. She too swam toward it, but down it went, and all the rose-colored glow faded from the sea and sky.

The following year, her third sister ascended, and as she was the boldest of them all she swam up a broad river that flowed into the ocean. She

saw gloriously green, vine-colored hills. Palaces and manor houses could be glimpsed through the splendid woods. She heard all the birds sing, and the sun shone so brightly that often she had to dive under the water to cool her burning face. In a small cove she found a whole school of mortal children, paddling about in the water quite naked. She wanted to play with them, but they took fright and ran away. Then along came a little black animal – it was a dog, but she had never seen a dog before. It barked at her so ferociously that she took fright herself, and fled to the open sea. But never could she forget the splendid woods, the green hills, and the nice children who could swim in the water although they didn't wear fish tails.

The fourth sister was not so venturesome. She stayed far out among the rough waves, which she said was a marvelous place. You could see all around you for miles and miles, and the heavens up above you were like a vast dome of glass. She had seen ships, but they were so far away that they looked like sea gulls. Playful dolphins had turned somersaults, and monstrous whales had spouted water through their nostrils so that it looked as if hundreds of fountains were playing all around them.

Now the fifth sister had her turn. Her birthday came in the wintertime, so she saw things that

none of the others had seen. The sea was a deep green color, and enormous icebergs drifted about.

Each one glistened like a pearl, she said, but they were more lofty than any church steeple built by man. They assumed the most fantastic shapes, and sparkled like diamonds. She had seated herself on the largest one, and all the ships that came sailing by sped away as soon as the frightened sailors saw her there with her long hair blowing in the wind.

In the late evening clouds filled the sky. Thunder cracked and lightning darted across the heavens. Black waves lifted those great bergs of ice on high, where they flashed when the lightning struck.

On all the ships the sails were reefed and there was fear and trembling. But quietly she sat there, upon her drifting iceberg, and watched the blue forked lightning strike the sea.

Each of the sisters took delight in the lovely new sights when she first rose up to the surface of the sea. But when they became grown-up girls, who were allowed to go wherever they liked, they became indifferent to it. They would become homesick, and in a month they said that there was no place like the bottom of the sea, where they felt so completely at home.

On many an evening the older sisters would rise

to the surface, arm in arm, all five in a row. They had beautiful voices, more charming than those of any mortal beings. When a storm was brewing, and they anticipated a shipwreck, they would swim before the ship and sing most seductively of how beautiful it was at the bottom of the ocean, trying to overcome the prejudice that the sailors had against coming down to them. But people could not understand their song, and mistook it for the voice of the storm. Nor was it for them to see the glories of the deep. When their ship went down they were drowned, and it was as dead men that they reached the sea king's palace.

On the evenings when the mermaids rose through the water like this, arm in arm, their youngest sister stayed behind all alone, looking after them and wanting to weep. But a mermaid has no tears, and therefore she suffers so much more.

"Oh, how I do wish I were fifteen!" she said. "I know I shall love that world up there and all the people who live in it."

And at last she too came to be fifteen.

"Now I'll have you off my hands," said her grandmother, the old queen dowager. "Come, let me adorn you like your sisters." In the little maid's hair she put a wreath of white lilies, each petal of which was formed from half of a pearl. And the old

queen let eight big oysters fasten themselves to the princess's tail, as a sign of her high rank.

"But that hurts!" said the little mermaid.

"You must put up with a good deal to keep up appearances," her grandmother told her.

Oh, how gladly she would have shaken off all these decorations, and laid aside the cumbersome wreath! The red flowers in her garden were much more becoming to her, but she didn't dare to make any changes. "Good-by," she said, and up she went through the water, as light and as sparkling as a bubble.

The sun had just gone down when her head rose above the surface, but the clouds still shone like gold and roses, and in the delicately tinted sky sparkled the clear gleam of the evening star. The air was mild and fresh and the sea unruffled. A great three-master lay in view with only one of all its sails set, for there was not even the whisper of a breeze, and the sailors idled about in the rigging and on the yards. There was music and singing on the ship, and as night came on they lighted hundreds of such brightly colored lanterns that one might have thought the flags of all nations were swinging in the air.

The little mermaid swam right up to the window of the main cabin, and each time she rose with the

swell she could peep in through the clear glass panes at the crowd of brilliantly dressed people within. The handsomest of them all was a young Prince with big dark eyes. He could not be more than sixteen years old. It was his birthday and that was the reason for all the celebration. Up on deck the sailors were dancing, and when the Prince appeared among them a hundred or more rockets flew through the air, making it as bright as day. These startled the little mermaid so badly that she ducked under the water. But she soon peeped up again, and then it seemed as if all the stars in the sky were falling around her. Never had she seen such fireworks. Great suns spun around, splendid fire-fish floated through the blue air, and all these things were mirrored in the crystal clear sea. It was so brilliantly bright that you could see every little rope of the ship, and the people could be seen distinctly. Oh, how handsome the young Prince was! He laughed, and he smiled and shook people by the hand, while the music rang out in the perfect evening.

It got very late, but the little mermaid could not take her eyes off the ship and the handsome Prince. The brightly colored lanterns were put out, no more rockets flew through the air, and no more cannon boomed. But there was a mutter and

rumble deep down in the sea, and the swell kept bouncing her up so high that she could look into the cabin.

Now the ship began to sail. Canvas after canvas was spread in the wind, the waves rose high, great clouds gathered, and lightning flashed in the distance. Ah, they were in for a terrible storm, and the mariners made haste to reef the sails. The tall ship pitched and rolled as it sped through the angry sea. The waves rose up like towering black mountains, as if they would break over the masthead, but the swan-like ship plunged into the valleys between such waves, and emerged to ride their lofty heights. To the little mermaid this seemed good sport, but to the sailors it was nothing of the sort. The ship creaked and labored, thick timbers gave way under the heavy blows, waves broke over the ship, the mainmast snapped in two like a reed, the ship listed over on its side, and water burst into the hold.

Now the little mermaid saw that people were in peril, and that she herself must take care to avoid the beams and wreckage tossed about by the sea. One moment it would be black as pitch, and she couldn't see a thing. Next moment the lightning would flash so brightly that she could distinguish every soul on board. Everyone was looking out for

himself as best he could. She watched closely for the young Prince, and when the ship split in two she saw him sink down in the sea. At first she was overjoyed that he would be with her, but then she recalled that human people could not live under the water, and he could only visit her father's palace as a dead man. No, he should not die! So she swam in among all the floating planks and beams, completely forgetting that they might crush her. She dived through the waves and rode their crests, until at length she reached the young Prince, who was no longer able to swim in that raging sea. His arms and legs were exhausted, his beautiful eyes were closing, and he would have died if the little mermaid had not come to help him. She held his head above water, and let the waves take them wherever the waves went.

At daybreak, when the storm was over, not a trace of the ship was in view. The sun rose out of the waters, red and bright, and its beams seemed to bring the glow of life back to the cheeks of the Prince, but his eyes remained closed. The mermaid kissed his high and shapely forehead. As she stroked his wet hair in place, it seemed to her that he looked like that marble statue in her little garden. She kissed him again and hoped that he would live.

She saw dry land rise before her in high blue mountains, topped with snow as glistening white as if a flock of swans were resting there. Down by the shore were splendid green woods, and in the foreground stood a church, or perhaps a convent; she didn't know which, but anyway it was a building. Orange and lemon trees grew in its garden, and tall palm trees grew beside the gateway. Here the sea formed a little harbor, quite calm and very deep. Fine white sand had been washed up below the cliffs. She swam there with the handsome Prince, and stretched him out on the sand, taking special care to pillow his head up high in the warm sunlight.

The bells began to ring in the great white building, and a number of young girls came out into the garden. The little mermaid swam away behind some tall rocks that stuck out of the water. She covered her hair and her shoulders with foam so that no one could see her tiny face, and then she watched to see who would find the poor Prince.

In a little while one of the young girls came upon him. She seemed frightened, but only for a minute; then she called more people. The mermaid watched the Prince regain consciousness, and smile at everyone around him. But he did not smile at her, for he did not even know that she had

saved him. She felt very unhappy, and when they led him away to the big building she dived sadly down into the water and returned to her father's palace.

She had always been quiet and wistful, and now she became much more so. Her sisters asked her what she had seen on her first visit up to the surface, but she would not tell them a thing.

Many evenings and many mornings she revisited the spot where she had left the Prince. She saw the fruit in the garden ripened and harvested, and she saw the snow on the high mountain melted away, but she did not see the Prince, so each time she came home sadder than she had left. It was her one consolation to sit in her little garden and throw her arms about the beautiful marble statue that looked so much like the Prince. But she took no care of her flowers now. They overgrew the paths until the place was a wilderness, and their long stalks and leaves became so entangled in the branches of the tree that it cast a gloomy shade.

Finally she couldn't bear it any longer. She told her secret to one of her sisters. Immediately all the other sisters heard about it. No one else knew, except a few more mermaids who told no one – except their most intimate friends. One of these

friends knew who the Prince was. She too had seen the birthday celebration on the ship. She knew where he came from and where his kingdom was.

"Come, little sister!" said the other princesses. Arm in arm, they rose from the water in a long row, right in front of where they knew the Prince's palace stood. It was built of pale, glistening, golden stone with great marble staircases, one of which led down to the sea. Magnificent gilt domes rose above the roof, and between the pillars all around the building were marble statues that looked most lifelike. Through the clear glass of the lofty windows one could see into the splendid halls, with their costly silk hangings and tapestries, and walls covered with paintings that were delightful to behold. In the center of the main hall a large fountain played its columns of spray up to the glass-domed roof, through which the sun shone down on the water and upon the lovely plants that grew in the big basin.

Now that she knew where he lived, many an evening and many a night she spent there in the sea. She swam much closer to shore than any of her sisters would dare venture, and she even went far up a narrow stream, under the splendid marble balcony that cast its long shadow in the water. Here she used to sit and watch the young Prince

when he thought himself quite alone in the bright moonlight.

On many evenings she saw him sail out in his fine boat, with music playing and flags a-flutter. She would peep out through the green rushes, and if the wind blew her long silver veil, anyone who saw it mistook it for a swan spreading its wings.

On many nights she saw the fishermen come out to sea with their torches, and heard them tell about how kind the young Prince was. This made her proud to think that it was she who had saved his life when he was buffeted about, half dead among the waves. And she thought of how softly his head had rested on her breast, and how tenderly she had kissed him, though he knew nothing of all this nor could he even dream of it.

Increasingly she grew to like human beings, and more and more she longed to live among them. Their world seemed so much wider than her own, for they could skim over the sea in ships, and mount up into the lofty peaks high over the clouds, and their lands stretched out in woods and fields farther than the eye could see. There was so much she wanted to know. Her sisters could not answer all her questions, so she asked her old grandmother, who knew about the "upper world," which

was what she said was the right name for the countries above the sea.

"If men aren't drowned," the little mermaid asked, "do they live on forever? Don't they die, as we do down here in the sea?"

"Yes," the old lady said, "they too must die, and their lifetimes are even shorter than ours. We can live to be three hundred years old, but when we perish we turn into mere foam on the sea, and haven't even a grave down here among our dear ones. We have no immortal soul, no life hereafter. We are like the green seaweed – once cut down, it never grows again. Human beings, on the contrary, have a soul which lives forever, long after their bodies have turned to clay. It rises through thin air, up to the shining stars. Just as we rise through the water to see the lands on earth, so men rise up to beautiful places unknown, which we shall never see."

"Why weren't we given an immortal soul?" the little mermaid sadly asked. "I would gladly give up my three hundred years if I could be a human being only for a day, and later share in that heavenly realm."

"You must not think about that," said the old lady. "We fare much more happily and are much better off than the folk up there."

"Then I must also die and float as foam upon the sea, not hearing the music of the waves, and seeing neither the beautiful flowers nor the red sun! Can't I do anything at all to win an immortal soul?"

"No," her grandmother answered, "not unless a human being loved you so much that you meant more to him than his father and mother. If his every thought and his whole heart cleaved to you so that he would let a priest join his right hand to yours and would promise to be faithful here and throughout all eternity, then his soul would dwell in your body, and you would share in the happiness of mankind. He would give you a soul and yet keep his own. But that can never come to pass. The very thing that is your greatest beauty here in the sea – your fish tail – would be considered ugly on land. They have such poor taste that to be thought beautiful there you have to have two awkward props which they call legs."

The little mermaid sighed and looked unhappily at her fish tail.

"Come, let us be gay!" the old lady said. "Let us leap and bound throughout the three hundred years that we have to live. Surely that is time and to spare, and afterwards we shall be glad enough

to rest in our graves. – We are holding a court ball this evening."

This was a much more glorious affair than is ever to be seen on earth. The walls and the ceiling of the great ballroom were made of massive but transparent glass. Many hundreds of huge rose-red and grass-green shells stood on each side in rows, with the blue flames that burned in each shell illuminating the whole room and shining through the walls so clearly that it was quite bright in the sea outside. You could see the countless fish, great and small, swimming toward the glass walls. On some of them the scales gleamed purplish-red, while others were silver and gold. Across the floor of the hall ran a wide stream of water, and upon this the mermaids and mermen danced to their own entrancing songs. Such beautiful voices are not to be heard among the people who live on land. The little mermaid sang more sweetly than anyone else, and everyone applauded her. For a moment her heart was happy, because she knew she had the loveliest voice of all, in the sea or on the land. But her thoughts soon strayed to the world up above. She could not forget the charming Prince, nor her sorrow that she did not have an immortal soul like his. Therefore she stole out of her father's palace and, while everything there was

song and gladness, she sat sadly in her own little garden.

Then she heard a bugle call through the water, and she thought, "That must mean he is sailing up there, he whom I love more than my father or mother, he of whom I am always thinking, and in whose hands I would so willingly trust my life-long happiness. I dare do anything to win him and to gain an immortal soul. While my sisters are dancing here, in my father's palace, I shall visit the sea witch of whom I have always been so afraid. Perhaps she will be able to advise me and help me."

The little mermaid set out from her garden toward the whirlpools that raged in front of the witch's dwelling. She had never gone that way before. No flowers grew there, nor any seaweed. Bare and gray, the sands extended to the whirlpools, where like roaring mill wheels the waters whirled and snatched everything within their reach down to the bottom of the sea. Between these tumultuous whirlpools she had to thread her way to reach the witch's waters, and then for a long stretch the only trail lay through a hot seething mire, which the witch called her peat marsh. Beyond it her house lay in the middle of a weird forest, where all the trees and shrubs were polyps, half animal

and half plant. They looked like hundred-headed snakes growing out of the soil. All their branches were long, slimy arms, with fingers like wriggling worms. They squirmed, joint by joint, from their roots to their outermost tentacles, and whatever they could lay hold of they twined around and never let go. The little mermaid was terrified, and stopped at the edge of the forest. Her heart thumped with fear and she nearly turned back, but then she remembered the Prince and the souls that men have, and she summoned her courage. She bound her long flowing locks closely about her head so that the polyps could not catch hold of them, folded her arms across her breast, and darted through the water like a fish, in among the slimy polyps that stretched out their writhing arms and fingers to seize her. She saw that every one of them held something that it had caught with its hundreds of little tentacles, and to which it clung as with strong hoops of steel. The white bones of men who had perished at sea and sunk to these depths could be seen in the polyps' arms. Ships' rudders, and seamen's chests, and the skeletons of land animals had also fallen into their clutches, but the most ghastly sight of all was a little mermaid whom they had caught and strangled.

She reached a large muddy clearing in the

forest, where big fat water snakes slithered about, showing their foul yellowish bellies. In the middle of this clearing was a house built of the bones of shipwrecked men, and there sat the sea witch, letting a toad eat out of her mouth just as we might feed sugar to a little canary bird. She called the ugly fat water snakes her little chickabiddies, and let them crawl and sprawl about on her spongy bosom.

"I know exactly what you want," said the sea witch. "It is very foolish of you, but just the same you shall have your way, for it will bring you to grief, my proud princess. You want to get rid of your fish tail and have two props instead, so that you can walk about like a human creature, and have the young Prince fall in love with you, and win him and an immortal soul besides." At this, the witch gave such a loud cackling laugh that the toad and the snakes were shaken to the ground, where they lay writhing. "You are just in time," said the witch. "After the sun comes up tomorrow, a whole year would have to go by before I could be of any help to you. I shall compound you a draft, and before sunrise you must swim to the shore with it, seat yourself on dry land, and drink the draft down. Then your tail will divide and shrink until it becomes what the people on earth call a pair

of shapely legs. But it will hurt; it will feel as if a sharp sword slashed through you. Everyone who sees you will say that you are the most graceful human being they have ever laid eyes on, for you will keep your gliding movement and no dancer will be able to tread as lightly as you. But every step you take will feel as if you were treading upon knife blades so sharp that blood must flow. I am willing to help you, but are you willing to suffer all this?" "Yes," the little mermaid said in a trembling voice, as she thought of the Prince and of gaining a human soul.

"Remember!" said the witch. "Once you have taken a human form, you can never be a mermaid again. You can never come back through the waters to your sisters, or to your father's palace. And if you do not win the love of the Prince so completely that for your sake he forgets his father and mother, cleaves to you with his every thought and his whole heart, and lets the priest join your hands in marriage, then you will win no immortal soul. If he marries someone else, your heart will break on the very next morning, and you will become foam of the sea."

"I shall take that risk," said the little mermaid, but she turned as pale as death.

"Also, you will have to pay me," said the witch,

"and it is no trifling price that I'm asking. You have the sweetest voice of anyone down here at the bottom of the sea, and while I don't doubt that you would like to captivate the Prince with it, you must give this voice to me. I will take the very best thing that you have, in return for my sovereign draft. I must pour my own blood in it to make the drink as sharp as a two-edged sword."

"But if you take my voice," said the little mermaid, "what will be left to me?"

"Your lovely form," the witch told her, "your gliding movements, and your eloquent eyes. With these you can easily enchant a human heart. Well, have you lost your courage? Stick out your little tongue and I shall cut it off. I'll have my price, and you shall have the potent draft."

"Go ahead," said the little mermaid.

The witch hung her caldron over the flames, to brew the draft. "Cleanliness is a good thing," she said, as she tied her snakes in a knot and scoured out the pot with them. Then she pricked herself in the chest and let her black blood splash into the caldron. Steam swirled up from it, in such ghastly shapes that anyone would have been terrified by them. The witch constantly threw new ingredients into the caldron, and it started to boil with a sound like that of a crocodile shedding tears. When the

draft was ready at last, it looked as clear as the purest water.

"There's your draft," said the witch. And she cut off the tongue of the little mermaid, who now was dumb and could neither sing nor talk.

"If the polyps should pounce on you when you walk back through my wood," the witch said, "just spill a drop of this brew upon them and their tentacles will break in a thousand pieces." But there was no need of that, for the polyps curled up in terror as soon as they saw the bright draft. It glittered in the little mermaid's hand as if it were a shining star. So she soon traversed the forest, the marsh, and the place of raging whirlpools.

She could see her father's palace. The lights had been snuffed out in the great ballroom, and doubtless everyone in the palace was asleep, but she dared not go near them, now that she was stricken dumb and was leaving her home forever. Her heart felt as if it would break with grief. She tip-toed into the garden, took one flower from each of her sisters' little plots, blew a thousand kisses toward the palace, and then mounted up through the dark blue sea.

The sun had not yet risen when she saw the Prince's palace. As she climbed his splendid marble staircase, the moon was shining clear. The

little mermaid swallowed the bitter, fiery draut, and it was as if a two-edged sword struck through her frail body. She swooned away, and lay there as if she were dead. When the sun rose over the sea she awoke and felt a flash of pain, but directly in front of her stood the handsome young Prince, gazing at her with his coal-black eyes. Lowering her gaze, she saw that her fish tail was gone, and that she had the loveliest pair of white legs any young maid could hope to have. But she was naked, so she clothed herself in her own long hair.

The Prince asked who she was, and how she came to be there. Her deep blue eyes looked at him tenderly but very sadly, for she could not speak. Then he took her hand and led her into his palace. Every footstep felt as if she were walking on the blades and points of sharp knives, just as the witch had foretold, but she gladly endured it. She moved as lightly as a bubble as she walked beside the Prince. He and all who saw her marveled at the grace of her gliding walk.

Once clad in the rich silk and muslin garments that were provided for her, she was the loveliest person in all the palace, though she was dumb and could neither sing nor speak. Beautiful slaves, attired in silk and cloth of gold, came to sing before the Prince and his royal parents. One of

them sang more sweetly than all the others, and when the Prince smiled at her and clapped his hands, the little mermaid felt very unhappy, for she knew that she herself used to sing much more sweetly.

"Oh," she thought, "if he only knew that I parted with my voice forever so that I could be near him."

Graceful slaves now began to dance to the most wonderful music. Then the little mermaid lifted her shapely white arms, rose up on the tips of her toes, and skimmed over the floor. No one had ever danced so well. Each movement set off her beauty to better and better advantage, and her eyes spoke more directly to the heart than any of the singing slaves could do.

She charmed everyone, and especially the Prince, who called her his dear little foundling. She danced time and again, though every time she touched the floor she felt as if she were treading on sharp-edged steel. The Prince said he would keep her with him always, and that she was to have a velvet pillow to sleep on outside his door.

He had a page's suit made for her, so that she could go with him on horseback. They would ride through the sweet scented woods, where the green

boughs brushed her shoulders, and where the little birds sang among the fluttering leaves.

She climbed up high mountains with the Prince, and though her tender feet bled so that all could see it, she only laughed and followed him on until they could see the clouds driving far below, like a flock of birds in flight to distant lands.

At home in the Prince's palace, while the others slept at night, she would go down the broad marble steps to cool her burning feet in the cold sea water, and then she would recall those who lived beneath the sea. One night her sisters came by, arm in arm, singing sadly as they breasted the waves. When she held out her hands toward them, they knew who she was, and told her how unhappy she had made them all. They came to see her every night after that, and once far, far out to sea, she saw her old grandmother, who had not been up to the surface this many a year. With her was the sea king, with his crown upon his head. They stretched out their hands to her, but they did not venture so near the land as her sisters had.

Day after day she became more dear to the Prince, who loved her as one would love a good little child, but he never thought of making her his Queen. Yet she had to be his wife or she would never have an immortal soul, and on the morning

after his wedding she would turn into foam on the waves.

"Don't you love me best of all?" the little mermaid's eyes seemed to question him, when he took her in his arms and kissed her lovely forehead.

"Yes, you are most dear to me," said the Prince, "for you have the kindest heart. You love me more than anyone else does, and you look so much like a young girl I once saw but never shall find again. I was on a ship that was wrecked, and the waves cast me ashore near a holy temple, where many young girls performed the rituals. The youngest of them found me beside the sea and saved my life. Though I saw her no more than twice, she is the only person in all the world whom I could love. But you are so much like her that you almost replace the memory of her in my heart. She belongs to that holy temple, therefore it is my good fortune that I have you. We shall never part."

"Alas, he doesn't know it was I who saved his life," the little mermaid thought. "I carried him over the sea to the garden where the temple stands. I hid behind the foam and watched to see if anyone would come. I saw the pretty maid he loves better than me." A sigh was the only sign of her deep distress, for a mermaid cannot cry. "He says that the

other maid belongs to the holy temple. She will never come out into the world, so they will never see each other again. It is I who will care for him, love him, and give all my life to him."

Now rumors arose that the Prince was to wed the beautiful daughter of a neighboring King, and that it was for this reason he was having such a superb ship made ready to sail. The rumor ran that the Prince's real interest in visiting the neighboring kingdom was to see the King's daughter, and that he was to travel with a lordly retinue. The little mermaid shook her head and smiled, for she knew the Prince's thoughts far better than anyone else did.

"I am forced to make this journey," he told her. "I must visit the beautiful Princess, for this is my parents' wish, but they would not have me bring her home as my bride against my own will, and I can never love her. She does not resemble the lovely maiden in the temple, as you do, and if I were to choose a bride, I would sooner choose you, my dear mute foundling with those telling eyes of yours." And he kissed her on the mouth, fingered her long hair, and laid his head against her heart so that she came to dream of mortal happiness and an immortal soul.

"I trust you aren't afraid of the sea, my silent

child," he said, as they went on board the magnificent vessel that was to carry them to the land of the neighboring King. And he told her stories of storms, of ships becalmed, of strange deep-sea fish, and of the wonders that divers have seen. She smiled at such stories, for no one knew about the bottom of the sea as well as she did.

In the clear moonlight, when everyone except the man at the helm was asleep, she sat on the side of the ship gazing down through the transparent water, and fancied she could catch glimpses of her father's palace. On the topmost tower stood her old grandmother, wearing her silver crown and looking up at the keel of the ship through the rushing waves. Then her sisters rose to the surface, looked at her sadly, and wrung their white hands. She smiled and waved, trying to let them know that all went well and that she was happy. But along came the cabin boy, and her sisters dived out of sight so quickly that the boy supposed the flash of white he had seen was merely foam on the sea.

Next morning the ship came in to the harbor of the neighboring King's glorious city. All the church bells chimed, and trumpets were sounded from all the high towers, while the soldiers lined up with flying banners and glittering bayonets. Every day

had a new festivity, as one ball or levee followed another, but the Princess was still to appear. They said she was being brought up in some far-away sacred temple, where she was learning every royal virtue. But she came at last.

The little mermaid was curious to see how beautiful this Princess was, and she had to grant that a more exquisite figure she had never seen. The Princess's skin was clear and fair, and behind the long, dark lashes her deep blue eyes were smiling and devoted.

"It was you!" the Prince cried. "You are the one who saved me when I lay like a dead man beside the sea." He clasped the blushing bride of his choice in his arms. "Oh, I am happier than a man should be!" he told his little mermaid. "My fondest dream – that which I never dared to hope – has come true. You will share in my great joy, for you love me more than anyone does."

The little mermaid kissed his hand and felt that her heart was beginning to break. For the morning after his wedding day would see her dead and turned to watery foam.

All the church bells rang out, and heralds rode through the streets to announce the wedding. Upon every altar sweet-scented oils were burned in costly silver lamps. The priests swung their censers,

the bride and the bridegroom joined their hands, and the bishop blessed their marriage. The little mermaid, clothed in silk and cloth of gold, held the bride's train, but she was deaf to the wedding march and blind to the holy ritual. Her thought turned on her last night upon earth, and on all she had lost in this world.

That same evening, the bride and bridegroom went aboard the ship. Cannon thundered and banners waved. On the deck of the ship a royal pavilion of purple and gold was set up, and furnished with luxurious cushions. Here the wedded couple were to sleep on that calm, clear night. The sails swelled in the breeze, and the ship glided so lightly that it scarcely seemed to move over the quiet sea. All nightfall brightly colored lanterns were lighted, and the mariners merrily danced on the deck. The little mermaid could not forget that first time she rose from the depths of the sea and looked on at such pomp and happiness. Light as a swallow pursued by his enemies, she joined in the whirling dance. Everyone cheered her, for never had she danced so wonderfully. Her tender feet felt as if they were pierced by daggers, but she did not feel it. Her heart suffered far greater pain. She knew that this was the last evening that she ever would see him for whom she had forsaken her

home and family, for whom she had sacrificed her lovely voice and suffered such constant torment, while he knew nothing of all these things. It was the last night that she would breathe the same air with him, or look upon deep waters or the star fields of the blue sky. A never-ending night, without thought and without dreams, awaited her who had no soul and could not get one. The merrymaking lasted long after midnight, yet she laughed and danced on despite the thought of death she carried in her heart. The Prince kissed his beautiful bride and she toyed with his coal-black hair. Hand in hand, they went to rest in the magnificent pavilion.

A hush came over the ship. Only the helmsman remained on deck as the little mermaid leaned her white arms on the bulwarks and looked to the east to see the first red hint of daybreak, for she knew that the first flash of the sun would strike her dead. Then she saw her sisters rise up among the waves. They were as pale as she, and there was no sign of their lovely long hair that the breezes used to blow. It had all been cut off.

"We have given our hair to the witch," they said, "so that she would send you help, and save you from death tonight. She gave us a knife. Here it is. See the sharp blade! Before the sun rises, you must

strike it into the Prince's heart, and when his warm blood bathes your feet they will grow together and become a fish tail. Then you will be a mermaid again, able to come back to us in the sea, and live out your three hundred years before you die and turn into dead salt sea foam. Make haste! He or you must die before sunrise. Our old grandmother is so grief-stricken that her white hair is falling fast, just as ours did under the witch's scissors. Kill the Prince and come back to us. Hurry! Hurry! See that red glow in the heavens! In a few minutes the sun will rise and you must die." So saying, they gave a strange deep sigh and sank beneath the waves.

The little mermaid parted the purple curtains of the tent and saw the beautiful bride asleep with her head on the Prince's breast. The mermaid bent down and kissed his shapely forehead. She looked at the sky, fast reddening for the break of day. She looked at the sharp knife and again turned her eyes toward the Prince, who in his sleep murmured the name of his bride. His thoughts were all for her, and the knife blade trembled in the mermaid's hand. But then she flung it from her, far out over the waves. Where it fell the waves were red, as if bubbles of blood seethed in the water. With eyes already glazing she looked once more at the

Prince, hurled herself over the bulwarks into the sea, and felt her body dissolve in foam.

The sun rose up from the waters. Its beams fell, warm and kindly, upon the chill sea foam, and the little mermaid did not feel the hand of death. In the bright sunlight overhead, she saw hundreds of fair ethereal beings. They were so transparent that through them she could see the ship's white sails and the red clouds in the sky. Their voices were sheer music, but so spirit-like that no human ear could detect the sound, just as no eye on earth could see their forms. Without wings, they floated as light as the air itself. The little mermaid discovered that she was shaped like them, and that she was gradually rising up out of the foam.

"Who are you, toward whom I rise?" she asked, and her voice sounded like those above her, so spiritual that no music on earth could match it.

"We are the daughters of the air," they answered. "A mermaid has no immortal soul, and can never get one unless she wins the love of a human being. Her eternal life must depend upon a power outside herself. The daughters of the air do not have an immortal soul either, but they can earn one by their good deeds. We fly to the south, where the hot poisonous air kills human beings

unless we bring cool breezes. We carry the scent of flowers through the air, bringing freshness and healing balm wherever we go. When for three hundred years we have tried to do all the good that we can, we are given an immortal soul and a share in mankind's eternal bliss. You, poor little mermaid, have tried with your whole heart to do this too. Your suffering and your loyalty have raised you up into the realm of airy spirits, and now in the course of three hundred years you may earn by your good deeds a soul that will never die."

The little mermaid lifted her clear bright eyes toward God's sun, and for the first time her eyes were wet with tears.

On board the ship all was astir and lively again. She saw the Prince and his fair bride in search of her. Then they gazed sadly into the seething foam, as if they knew she had hurled herself into the waves. Unseen by them, she kissed the bride's forehead, smiled upon the Prince, and rose up with the other daughters of the air to the rose-red clouds that sailed on high.

"This is the way that we shall rise to the kingdom of God, after three hundred years have passed."

"We may get there even sooner," one spirit whispered. "Unseen, we fly into the homes of men,

where there are children, and for every day on which we find a good child who pleases his parents and deserves their love, God shortens our days of trial. The child does not know when we float through his room, but when we smile at him in approval one year is taken from our three hundred. But if we see a naughty, mischievous child we must shed tears of sorrow, and each tear adds a day to the time of our trial."

MACMILLAN COLLECTOR'S LIBRARY

Own the world's great works of literature in one beautiful collectible library

Designed and curated to appeal to book lovers everywhere, Macmillan Collector's Library editions are small enough to travel with you and striking enough to take pride of place on your bookshelf. These much-loved literary classics also make the perfect gift.

Beautifully made, every Macmillan Collector's Library book adheres to the same high production values. Each hardback features gilt edges, a ribbon marker and cloth binding, and every paperback has a bespoke illustrated cover.

Discover a new and exciting anthology or cherish your favourite classic stories with this elegant collection.

Macmillan Collector's Library: own, collect, and treasure

Discover the full range at
panmacmillan.com/mcl